This *Elegant* RUIN

and other stories

ERIN BARTELS

Understory Press

THIS ELEGANT RUIN... AND OTHER STORIES

Copyright © 2014 by Erin Bartels

Published by Understory Press – Lansing, Michigan

This is a work of fiction. Names, characters, places, and
incidents are the product of the author's imagination or are
used fictitiously, and any resemblance to actual persons,
living or dead, events, or locations is entirely coincidental.

"This Elegant Ruin" first appeared in the online portion of
the *Saturday Evening Post* in January 2014.

For Mom and Dad,
who have always encouraged me…
in everything.

CONTENTS

Author's Note

In December of 2012, I was coming off a year or so of working on a failed novel. I didn't have the ideas—didn't have the heart—to start another right away, but I was looking for a way to keep myself writing fiction regularly as I waited patiently for the long-form muse to stop sulking and start speaking. Quite out of the blue I had an idea to write one short story each month of 2013 and to start submitting to magazines and journals, as well as self-publish them— not so much for profit, but in order to make myself reach my self-imposed deadlines.

So I announced my big plans to some very lovely people who read my blog, telling them that each month a new story would be available to download for their e-readers, and that at some point I'd collect them all in a print version for those who are not passengers on the ebook train.

In the meantime, I was also finding various contests to enter, including the Great American Fiction Contest run by the *Saturday Evening Post*. To my great delight, the lead story in this collection, "This Elegant Ruin," was a finalist for that award. It was available through the online portion of their magazine and was also included in the subsequent anthology. It was a much-needed confidence booster that came at just the right time.

Through my year of writing one short story every month, I explored several genres, different points of view, and varied settings. However, the attentive reader may surmise that the stories all have one thing in common—namely, that they are all set in Michigan.

Three are set in Detroit: "This Elegant Ruin," "One Endless Summer Day," and "Memory Man." Two are set in Michigan's gloriously undeveloped Upper Peninsula or UP (pronounced YOO-PEE, not "up"): "Drive" and "The Astonishing Moment." Others are set in rural hamlets, small town municipal buildings, or the ubiquitous county fair. You'll notice that highways and forests and fields feature heavily in some, home and family and career in others. Every season is represented and weather often sets the mood.

The experience of writing all of these stories in one year is one that changed me. It is my hope that, as you read them, you will find a few that change you too—even if the change is simply that you pay closer attention to a summer breeze or that you find the good, however small, lurking within the things that go wrong in life.

Thanks for reading.

THIS ELEGANT RUIN

Garrison Knight reached into the vast body of air before him as far as his stiff, tailored jacket would allow. Beneath the powerful lights above, tiny specks of dust waited for the fourth movement to begin so they could continue their shivery aerial dance. His fingers positioned as though he held a delicate china teacup in each hand, he took a slow breath then rose up on the balls of his wingtip shoes, opened his eyes wide, and flicked his wrists.

Instantly into the silence burst forth a vibrating, humming, menacing sound formed from a sea of strings and resonance chambers of varnished spruce and maple. Assertive and insistent, the sound lapped then crashed against the shoreline of rapt listeners like the waves of a stirred up ocean. Then the horns sang out their answer, a powerful blast of confidence like a whirlwind. The sounds mixed and mingled, a storm of symphonic elements lashing the audience. Swirling, churning, crashing for a moment until the bottom suddenly dropped out and there was a tenuous calm.

The white locks of unkempt hair that had been blowing about in the tempest settled back onto Garrison's forehead as he gently plucked sweet sentiments from oboes, flutes, and violins with his left hand. With the right, he pulled beautiful round phrases from the rows of shining brass, and with a nod came the deep emotions of cello and bass. Drawing his hands ever closer to his chest, Garrison pressed the sounds into a sphere, slowly packing them tighter and tighter, like a snowball. Then all at once he released them again and the dust-speckled air above the orchestra thrummed with energy for the space of a few more breaths.

Garrison gave his musicians the freedom to launch this sonic assault on the audience for a space, then deftly pulled them back down into their seats once more and laid the sound out like a cloth upon a broad table. He patted it down, flattening the wrinkled peaks of notes until it was completely smooth. Then he closed his eyes as if in prayer before a meal.

Suddenly he clutched at the sound and snapped it in the air. The instruments screamed. Garrison's cheeks shook and his entire upper body convulsed with energy, though his feet remained planted, a tree, unshifting, solid against the thrashing storm. *Rat-a-tat-tat, rat-a-tat-tat, rat-a-tat-tat, rat-a-tat-tat. Boom...boom... boommmmmm.*

Then silence, like a stopped heart. Thunderous applause. And Garrison breathed again. He glanced over his beloved musicians, his eyes smiling though his mouth remained a tight line. It had been a wonderful performance—one of their very best—and he was proud.

He turned to the audience and did his customary bows. He motioned to the various sections of the orchestra and caused particular musicians to rise with a small wave of his hand. But as they always did during the past several performances, his eyes lingered longest on a young violinist with long hair the color of ripe winter wheat and a creamy complexion, though she had never played a special part or a solo.

When the curtain closed, Anna stood and gathered up her music and her violin. The sound of chairs scraping against the floor and music stands being lowered and the drone of the audience talking excitedly about where to go for a late-night bite of dessert now filled the space of the hall, and the bits of lively dust disappeared as the spotlights were lost and the stage dimmed.

Garrison's all-powerful hands, which had commanded this precise aural army like a puppet master controlled his marionettes, were now grasped and shaken by these people who were, once again, just people. Some pudgy, some homely, some sweating, some awkward. A tall man, Garrison watched over their heads as Anna's long hair disappeared backstage.

Back in the green room the musicians were chatting and mingling, drinking the complimentary coffee and nibbling cookies. Garrison scanned the room for that lovely hair, but just when he located Anna, a man pushed a microphone into his face and another turned a large video camera on him.

"Mr. Knight," the man said through a wide grin, "can I get you to say a few words about tonight's performance?"

"Of course," Garrison replied, though with some hesitation. He knew what was coming.

"Simply wonderful performance, sir, and I'm sure you're happy with how your orchestra has handled Dvořák's 9th. But can you tell us why you chose the New World Symphony as your last piece for tonight's performance?"

"Certainly." Garrison launched into his memorized response to such questions from the local media. They always wanted to know why he had chosen the music he had. As if he could explain it to them somehow. Still, he always managed to give them some sort of fake little explanation they could quote in their articles or use to fill up a few seconds of air time on a slow news day.

Then came the second question he had expected.

"I understand that tonight's performance was your last for a while. What will these musicians—and you yourself—do during the strike and what do you hope to accomplish with this strike?"

Again, Garrison spoke on autopilot. He reiterated the rationale the symphony had for striking, gave a little history of the venerable organization to put it all in context, and said that though they would not be coming together to practice during the strike that they, being musicians, would all find ways to use their gifts and talents during this downtime and come back all the more energized and full of passion when the strike ended.

All during this speech, Garrison watched Anna from a distance. He watched as she spoke with her fellow musicians. Watched as not a few men flirted with her and offered to refill her Styrofoam coffee cup. Watched as she checked the delicate silver watch on her wrist. For a moment their eyes met across the room and she smiled politely then looked away. She seemed tired.

When Garrison finally escaped the reporter, he began working his way across the room, shaking hands and chatting rather mindlessly as he went. Each time he began to make progress, someone else would stop him. One grasped his arm, another held up a hand and beckoned, and still another simply swept in to block his path. When he finally reached the place where Anna had stood, the spot had been taken up by a tiresome cellist he loathed. Garrison spun on his heels to avoid eye contact then searched the room, aware that he must look a bit like a teenager desperate to find someone special at a school dance but not quite caring enough to be more subtle.

He stuck his head out the door and heard the tinkling of metal hangers around the corner. Following the sound, Garrison saw the back of Anna's head as she flipped her long hair out from her jacket collar and walked quickly on high-heeled shoes toward the exit. Garrison hesitated a moment at the coat rack, but at the sight of dozens of nearly identical black coats he gave up and headed for the door Anna had just gone through.

In the parking ramp stairwell he stopped and listened for footsteps. *Tap, tap, tap.* He grabbed the cool metal railing and followed the sound upward. As he reached the third level, the tapping stopped and he started taking the remaining stairs two at a time. He heard the pressing of a crash bar and the squeak of a heavy metal door, then felt a blast of cold air and chased it. At the fourth level he pushed through the same door onto the roof of the parking ramp and saw Anna ahead of him silhouetted against the night sky, violin case in hand, shoulders hunched against a cold drizzle.

At the sound of his approach she quickened her pace, but after all those stairs Garrison had to catch his breath.

"Miss Easton!" he called.

Anna turned and squinted at him.

"Oh! Mr. Knight!" She walked back toward him a few paces holding her free hand over her heart. "I didn't realize it was you."

"I'm sorry, Miss Easton. I didn't mean to alarm you."

Together they closed the distance between them until they stood face to face. For a moment neither of them spoke. Anna waited for him to say something, but Garrison hadn't managed to think of what he wanted to say in all the time he had been following her. She raised her eyebrows slightly to prompt him.

"Uh, yes. Miss Easton, I just wanted a chance to thank you for your work over the past few months. You're an excellent addition to our group. I don't always have a chance to say such things. But I did want you to know how much you are appreciated."

Anna smiled. "Thank you, sir."

Garrison watched the drizzle accumulate on Anna's hair, shimmering like dew in the glow of a nearby lamppost, and the silence stretched on between them.

"It is a beautiful piece of music," Anna said to fill the void.

"Yes, it is. It's always been one of my favorites."

A siren sounded in the distance.

"So," Garrison fumbled, "what will you do during the strike?"

"I'm in a band, actually, so I'll probably be doing more shows with them."

"A band?"

"Yeah, it's called SlapDash. It's sort of a folk punk thing. We play in small clubs around town. Just a hobby for most of us, though Ryan is pretty serious about it."

"Ryan?"

"Our lead guitarist."

Garrison tried to take this in. Folk punk? What exactly was that?

"You play the violin in this band?"

She smiled. "No, I'm the bassist."

"Oh," was all he managed for a moment. "Is this acoustic?"

"Electric, mostly. Some acoustic now and then. A little banjo occasionally. Think The Violent Femmes, only faster."

Garrison nodded slowly as though the name held some meaning for him.

"What about you?" Anna said.

"Me?"

"What will you be doing during the strike?"

"Oh." Garrison winced a little thinking of how he would no doubt be filling his time. "I imagine I'll be called on to do a few interviews, answering questions, meeting with lawyers. Things like that."

"Sounds fun," she quipped.

Garrison shook his head. "It's the worst part of it all. Dragged around from studio to studio, some reporter or talk show host picking at you, trying to get you to say something profound or at least something stupid so they can twist it on you. A circus, really. But I'm afraid I don't really have much choice."

Anna looked at him with sympathetic eyes. "Bummer."

"I'll work on some arrangements for when we all return, perhaps," he added, though only because he didn't want this young woman feeling sorry for him. Lately he hadn't been able to muster much enthusiasm for writing parts.

"Will you miss conducting?"

"Yes, I think so. Though I've been considering retirement lately." Garrison saw what he hoped he correctly interpreted as disappointment in Anna's face. "Of course, that's far from certain. I would miss seeing all your lovely faces."

He held her gaze a bit longer than was comfortable for either of them and they each looked away, he at his now quite damp tails, she at her violin case. Her hair was wet through now, the dewy bits of drizzle having found one another and coalesced.

"I'm sorry," Garrison said. "I shouldn't be keeping you out here in the cold rain. I just didn't want you to leave without—"

He stopped talking then because he didn't know what to say.

Anna smiled again and held out her hand to him. "It's an honor playing for you, sir," she said as he took her wet hand in his and shook it firmly. "I hope the strike won't last long."

"Yes, me too. You will be coming back, won't you?"

"Yes. Well, that is, I think so. I may end up going on the road a bit with the band and if things go well I guess it's possible I won't be able to get back. Can't be two places at once."

Garrison's heart began to panic in his chest. "I thought you said that was just a hobby."

"At the moment. But who knows, you know? I've got my whole life ahead of me. Gotta follow it where it leads. Thanks, again, Mr. Knight. I'm sure I'll be seeing you soon."

She turned and walked to her car then and Garrison turned back toward the stairwell. After the sound of her car door shutting and the engine revving to life, he heard a muffled cacophony of guitars and drums and the whine of a voice that sounded like a cassette tape left too many summers in a hot car.

Garrison watched the reflection of her brake lights on the concrete until she turned the corner and headed down the ramp, then he walked to the edge of the lot and peered down to the street below. His wet hair hanging limply in his face, he looked at the spot on the road where she would appear and then followed her car with his eyes as she headed east toward the place where the sun would rise in a little less than eight hours. When he couldn't see it anymore, he turned away and went into the stairwell.

The door clicked behind him and he leaned against the cold cinder block wall. He looked at his wet shoes, released a low sigh, and slowly made his way back down the stairs to the main level. He had to find his keys. He had to go back in to sift through the black coats. He had to get out of these wet clothes. He had to face tomorrow.

During the weeks and months that followed as the strike wore on, Garrison muddled his way through the day-to-day business of living. Each evening when the sun set, he found himself wondering where Anna might be. What was her band called?

Flash Dance? Where might they play? Garrison's musical world had been so insulated from the sort of popular noise that most people seemed to prefer over classical music, he didn't even know what bars or clubs might have live bands.

Then one day as he thumbed mindlessly through some free newspaper found left on a coffee shop table, he saw it. SlapDash. That's what it was. They were playing that evening in a bar in a particularly blighted section of a city that was becoming world-renowned for its spectacular fall into ruin. Garrison found it difficult to imagine the tall, slender, and elegant Anna wielding an electric bass in a room full of half-drunken people who were likely all concealing guns beneath their jackets.

He took the paper home with him and laid it on the kitchen counter next to the coffeepot. He made a few phone calls, sat at his piano, tried to work on a piece, but his mind kept straying to that little notice in the paper. After a dinner of eggs and toast, Garrison made up his mind to go to the club.

He put on his only pair of jeans and a sweater over a white dress shirt, slipped a pocketknife into his pocket, and pulled on his overcoat and scarf. A glance in the hall mirror told him that, try as he might to blend in, he would still seem out of place at almost any Detroit bar. But the thought of seeing Anna again drove him out the door and down darkened, snowy streets the city had given up on. After some doubling back and a heart-stoppingly long red light near a barred-up gas station in Redford that seemed to be a beacon for drug dealers, he reached his destination.

Trash and cigarette butts peppered the cracked and icy sidewalk and Garrison's untrained eye could not tell whether the graffiti that graced the walls was purposeful artwork or the calling card of a gang of hoodlums. He parked as close as he could and walked briskly through the cold. Every muscle in his body seemed to tug at him, urging him to come to his senses and turn around. But he forced his hand to open the door.

A burst of dissonance assaulted him and he would have shut the door again had it not been flung all the way open by a heavily tattooed and sneering young woman on her way out. Steeling himself, Garrison walked in then fumbled a moment for his wallet to pay the cover charge. He searched the crowded room for somewhere to sit, but settled for leaning on a bit of wall where he had a fairly unobstructed view of the small stage.

The music blared through enormous amplifiers stacked on either side of the band. To an ear attuned over decades to the slightest nuances of volume and tone, the sound spewing forth from the stage was painful. Behind the drum set, Garrison saw a man walloping each drum and cymbal as if he were cutting down a tree with a dull ax. The sounds that were being scraped from the lead guitar set Garrison's teeth on edge, and the rhythm guitarist and the drummer seemed to be having a dispute about the tempo.

When he finally caught a glimpse of Anna over the crowd, he hardly recognized her. Her eyes were lidded in heavy black makeup, her lips a deep red, her beautiful hair streaked with blue and gathered into two low pigtails. Instead of the elegant black dress she wore to performances with the symphony, she wore tight jeans tucked into tall black leather boots and a tiny black tank top that said "GIRL" in shiny purple rhinestones. Her bass guitar slung low across her narrow hips, Anna occasionally stepped up to a microphone to harmonize with the lead guitarist as he spat out nearly unintelligible lyrics, but the rest of the time she kept her head down.

A waitress with a tray full of empty beer bottles and glasses edged past Garrison to get behind the bar and then suddenly noticed he was there.

"Need a drink?" she shouted at him.

Garrison shook his head slightly.

"You sure?" she bellowed. "You look like you need to relax."

Once more he shook his head and then turned his attention back to the stage. A moment later, the waitress handed him a glass of something.

"It's on me," she said. "Give it a try."

Garrison stood against the wall for the next forty-five minutes nursing the drink. It didn't make the music any better, but it did blur some of the harsh lines of sight and sound enough so that he could almost stand it. He never took his eyes off of Anna and, as he tuned his ears to the low sounds of the bass and watched her fingers fly effortlessly over the strings, he managed to appreciate her contribution despite his distaste for the whole.

Finally the set was finished. The band members waved to the rather indifferent crowd and stepped down off the low stage to become part of it. Though more than one guy tried to waylay her, Anna elbowed her way up to the bar and asked the bartender for a club soda. Garrison watched her from his spot on the wall as she leaned on the bar, snatched an ice cube from her glass, then popped it into her mouth and crushed it between her teeth.

Someone on the other side of Anna caught her up in a conversation and she turned away from Garrison. With her hair parted and her shoulders bare, Garrison could now see that sprawled across Anna's upper back was the tattoo of a large bird, its wings outstretched and reaching almost from one shoulder to the other.

It was at this moment that Garrison realized that perhaps this was not the right setting to talk again with Anna. She might find it strange for him to have tracked her down and lurked in a corner all night waiting for an opportunity to talk to her. He quickly set his empty glass down at the end of the bar and walked behind Anna toward the door, the end of his scarf brushing across the tip of that tattooed bird's wing.

Anna looked up at the retreating figure. The only one in the room in a trench coat. The only one in the room with white hair. She stood and pushed her way through the crowd to the door that had just slammed shut behind the man. Opening it again, she was greeted by large snowflakes falling straight down. She looked up and down the shadowy street and spotted him.

"Mr. Knight?" Anna called down the dark sidewalk.

Garrison stopped at her voice and turned. Anna trotted toward him in those tall boots, hugging her bare arms against the snow and cold.

"Mr. Knight, I thought that was you," she said.

"Ah, Miss Easton. Yes. I saw your band playing here tonight and I just thought I would swing by to see what you sounded like."

This close to her now, Garrison saw the sparkle of a small nose ring just above her right nostril. Had that always been there?

"Yeah, and what did you think?" she asked. "I know it's kind of night and day to the symphony."

"You are a very good bass player."

"Thanks," she said with a small smile.

"It was...louder than I expected."

Anna laughed at this. "Yeah, it's pretty loud."

They looked at one another a moment and said nothing as the snow fell silently past their faces.

"Your hair," Garrison said.

Anna looked a bit sheepish. "It's not permanent. Figured since I wasn't playing symphonies I could look more the part of the punk rocker. Fits the image of the band a little better."

Garrison nodded slightly. "It was really quite lovely the way you had it before."

A blush crept into Anna's cheeks. "Thanks, Mr. Knight. Don't worry. I'll change it back if I ever play for you again."

Garrison smiled sadly at her.

"Any news of the strike ending?" she asked.

"I think we may be getting a little closer," he said. "But I fear I may be getting too old for this sort of nonsense."

"You're not really thinking of retiring, are you?" Anna said as she rubbed her upper arms.

Garrison nodded again. "Maybe. Not sure I've got it in me anymore. I'm feeling a bit run down, like this whole town."

Anna pressed her lips together and nodded as well. "I'm thinking of getting out of Detroit. Maybe go to California or something. Somewhere warmer."

"Where are my manners, Miss Easton. I'm sorry. Please take my coat. You must be freezing." He shrugged out of his trench coat and placed it over her shoulders before she could protest, shrouding the great bird across her back in darkness.

"Thanks," she said.

After a moment of awkward silence, Garrison asked, "What is your tattoo? An eagle?"

Anna looked a little embarrassed. "A phoenix. I know it's crazy big. It was a college thing."

"No, that's neat. A phoenix. Rises from the ashes anew. I like that."

"Thanks," she said again.

Garrison gazed at her a moment. She looked so small in his big coat. A girl in pigtails quickly gathering snow. And he was not a young man anymore.

"You better get back inside," he said in a fatherly tone, "and I had better get home. It's way past my bedtime."

He walked her back to the door of the bar and she handed him his coat.

"It was good to see you again, Anna."

"You too, Mr. Knight."

Garrison opened the door and Anna was once more swallowed up by the crowd and the noise. He walked to his car, drove back home through the dark night, and sat at his kitchen table until the gray light in the east told him the sun would soon rise.

BENEATH THE WINTER WEEDS

The moment Valerie Steele hung up the phone she knew it was time to plan one last trip to the old woods behind her grandmother's house. Now that the ancient woman was buried in the frosty January ground and the estate sale was complete, Valerie's mother was putting the old white house up for sale. Soon prospective buyers would be clomping through those hallowed rooms, scuffing up her grandmother's perfectly waxed floors, and yanking at the drawers in the kitchen.

It made her a little sad to think of never staying in that house again, never again eating cookies at the kitchen table, never walking quickly by the door that led to the dark basement with the damp dirt floor. And yet it was not the house itself that she felt compelled to see one last time. There was something waiting for her in the woods, and this would be her last chance to make the pilgrimage she had always known she would need to make someday.

She woke before dawn the next morning and pulled on two pairs of warm socks, layered leggings underneath her jeans, and piled on a tank top, a t-shirt, a long-sleeved tee, a sweater, and her heavy wool winter coat. She shoved her feet into her winter boots, wrapped a scarf around her neck, and sheathed her hands in two pairs of gloves. It was just sixteen degrees Fahrenheit outside and she had a long walk ahead of her.

Tossing a banana on the passenger seat and placing her travel mug of coffee in the cup holder, Valerie pulled out of the parking lot of her building just as the stars were beginning to fade in that soft moment before the sun breaks over the horizon. She drove to the highway, then sped east past housing developments and stubbled cornfields until she reached exit 52 where she headed north through rolling farmland.

The sun was a glowing orange orb that looked far warmer than it felt as Valerie finally parked her car on her grandmother's gravel driveway a few miles off the interstate and got out into the clear, frozen air. She retrieved a small, folding metal camp shovel from her trunk and put it in her oversized coat pocket. As she crunched across the crusted snow toward the western woods, the sun crested the windbreak behind her and the trees ahead blazed like burnished bronze. Tall dried grasses at the edges of the woods glowed gold and the clouded western sky beyond was pewter. She followed her shadow to the faint path her own childish feet had cut years before and stepped among the stately, naked trees.

Having taken this route nearly every day after school for a decade or more, she knew it better than any other place she had ever been. Better than the halls of her high school. Better than her college campus. Better even than the airport terminals she found herself haunting so often now as she traveled from city to city.

Still, she had not been in these woods for almost fifteen years and, as forests are wont to do, they had changed. As a girl, Valerie recognized every tree along this winding thread of matted plants and dried pine needles. Her soft fingers had worn smooth the bark of saplings and stumps as she braced herself at a dip or hauled herself up out of a small ravine. But now the saplings of her youth were towering giants and the stumps had been reclaimed by the earth. Some of the oldest trees had bowed to wind, cracked and split as they became stiff with age and could no longer take the storms in stride, and now blocked her path where it had been clear years before. As she pressed onward through the trees, she found herself hesitating, second guessing, retracing then pressing on.

Instinct drove her on from one end. Knowing what might lay beyond the ravine, somewhere beneath the ground, drew her ever closer from the other. Like a drop of rain upon a long blade of wild grass, she was inching ever closer to the root of it all. And when she at last came to the ravine and began a careful descent on the frozen ground, she had a palpable sense of acceleration, of reaching the point of no return.

She walked gingerly alongside the trickle of still-running water at the bottom of the ravine, her eyes searching for the natural staircase of gnarled roots she knew was to come. By this time the sun was higher and thinner and the trees had lost their glow. Strong shadows lay like bars across the snow and the pale blue sky above quivered with ice crystals. Her breath intermittently clouded her view. A few minutes more and she saw the roots leading up the far slope. She gripped them, dug the toes of her boots into the loose leaves and snow, and pulled herself slowly up the steep embankment.

When she reached the top she tensed and straightened, then looked back the way she'd just come. In her youth it had seemed such an easy thing to scamper up and down, like leaping up the porch steps at the end of the day. Now seeing just how far a climb and how great a drop it was onto the rocky creek bed below, Valerie knew the shiver that came over her had nothing to do with the temperature.

All at once she felt profoundly alone. Isolated. Cut off. As a girl she had loved to be on her own in the woods, had cherished every blessedly quiet and sacred moment by herself, without the judging eyes of her peers boring into her, without the critical assessment of her mother. To be alone then was to be herself, truly, wholly.

Her grandmother had always understood it. When Valerie breezed into the house at twilight, breathless and filthy and ready for dinner, her mother at work or out with friends or simply too frazzled to deal with her, Grandma was slow to speak but a ready listener. She would draw her granddaughter's adventures from her with a well-placed smile and eyes that twinkled with latent mischief. Valerie would recount the minute details of her day: every flower that had caught her eye, every bird's thrilling song, every glimpse of a deer. She held nothing back—until the autumn her father showed up quite unexpectedly and quite uninvited.

She had come home from school to find her grandmother sitting primly in the rarely used living room with a strange man Valerie had never seen. After an awkward introduction, she followed her grandmother into the kitchen to freshen the man's coffee. The old woman leaned close to Valerie's ear and told her that as long as the man was there she was to remain in sight of the house at all times. No gallivanting off to the woods. It would be rude to leave a guest like that, she had said. So Valerie resigned herself to an undisclosed time of trying to conjure up some enthusiasm for more domestic pursuits.

The man hung around for a week or so, appearing in doorways and around the corner of the garage. It always made Valerie start to see him. Hers was a world of women and she squirmed under this strange man's quizzical gaze. Her mother and grandmother were sure to keep an eye on her when her father was around, making obvious noise in the next room or finding excuses to stay by Valerie's side. It wasn't that they had thought her father was dangerous, she had decided years later as she considered that exceptional autumn. It was simply that he was a stranger.

When she asked her mother why he was there she was told that he was just passing through on his way to a job and that he would be leaving soon. And yet, there he would be again the next day, sitting on the porch or at the kitchen table. He didn't talk much and he never spoke directly to Valerie, and so she never spoke to him. Then, after days of tense silence, he was gone. Off to the job. And she was once again allowed to play in the woods.

Thrilled to be loosed into the wild, she hardly got her tennis shoes tied and her sweater on before she burst out the back door and shot across the yard at full speed for the opening in the woods. She tore through the trees toward the ravine, reveling in the crisp air, the crunch of yellow leaves beneath her feet, and the smell of burning wood drifting on the breeze from a distant farm. She leapt over logs and rocks and startled birds and expertly slid down the side of the ravine like a seasoned surfer riding a wave. When her feet hit the bottom she made her way down the ravine to the staircase of roots, effortlessly leaping back and forth over the creek. Then she scampered up the tree roots with no more thought than she gave to brushing her teeth, automatically positioning her hands and feet where she always did.

So rote and natural were her actions that she nearly wasn't able to stop herself as she crested the top. From there she would normally have taken the path through the pines to a little clearing in the woods where the goldenrods, teasel, asters, and Queen Anne's lace bloomed. But that day the path was blocked by a man, his shadow just grazing her fingers as she crouched at the edge of the ravine. She hung there, indecisive. Before she had quite decided to lower herself back down the root system to try to sneak back the way she had come, the man's boots filled her field of vision.

"Valerie?"

Her father held his hand out to her. As there was nothing else to do, she took it and he drew her up out of the ravine. She met his eyes, new and yet familiar, but could not speak.

"What are you doing way out here?" he asked.

She gave a tiny shake of her head and whispered, "Nothing."

For the first time since he had showed up, he smiled at her. "That's kind of what I'm doing too."

Now on this cold January day as she stood on the very spot, crusted over with winter as it was, Valerie felt the old emotions creep up her legs from the forest floor and settle in the pit of her stomach. Fear. Curiosity. Suspicion. Longing. Then she started forward toward the clearing just beyond the belt of pines. Crunching over the snow, she could almost feel his presence beside her as on that golden autumn day.

"I was just out here taking a walk," he had said. "I saw some flowers over this way and I thought I'd bring some back to your mom. Want to help me pick some?"

"Sure," she had said, though she had always before obeyed her grandmother's admonishment not to pick the flowers she found in the woods. Some were rare, some were poisonous, and all were placed there for a reason. "Let's not uproot what God has planted," her grandmother would say. But somehow Valerie didn't think of passing this wisdom on to the man who walked beside her through the towering pines.

When they came to the clearing she smiled to herself despite her uncertainty. This was her favorite spot in the woods. Her enchanted meadow. This was where the fairies lived. This was where her imagination swelled and ideas and stories broke free like the fresh green shoots of well-planted seeds. This was where butterflies and bees and clouds of tiny insects congregated and made the very air around her thrum with life. She looked over the rich tableau of golden yellow, creamy white, deep purple, and pale violet and was quite suddenly thrilled with the idea of picking, arranging, creating a miniature version of this wondrous display of color to bring back to the white house. Her grandmother had surely never been out to see it and, try as she might, Valerie's descriptions of the place couldn't possibly be enough for the uninitiated to correctly picture it. None of these particular flowers were rare or poisonous; this she knew. Surely it wouldn't hurt just this once.

The two of them wandered in separate directions around the clearing, Valerie pinching off asters with her sharp fingernails, her father slicing through the tough stems of goldenrod and Queen Anne's lace with his pocketknife. When each of them had a good handful they meandered back around toward each other. The man handed her his bunch and she fiddled with them until she was pleased with the mix of colors.

"Looks good," he said. He motioned back the way they had come. "Shall we?"

Valerie looked at the bouquet.

"What about the teasel?"

"The what?"

"The teasel," she repeated. "Those." She pointed to a clump of tall, spiky plants that looked more like the burnt remains of a prehistoric forest than flowers.

"Those things?" he asked.

She nodded.

"Those are just weeds."

"No they're not. They're wildflowers."

"No, they're weeds. Look at them. They're brown and dead, anyway."

"Weeds are only weeds in a garden when you didn't plant them and you don't want them. Those are wildflowers and I think Mom would like them."

He shrugged. "Whatever you say."

They headed to the opposite side of the clearing to the patch of teasel. While Valerie stood by, her father made an attempt to cut some off with his knife but the rigid spikes lining the stems pricked his palms and he swore. He looked around at the trees.

"Hold on a second. Just let me get something for my hands." He looked down at her again. "You sure we need these?"

She nodded and he headed for a stand of birch trees. Valerie watched him go then looked back at the teasel. Her eyes focused on a large granite boulder beyond the dried flower heads. Beside the rock was a patch of disturbed ground. The dirt was mounded up, about a foot wide, and felt damp to her fingers when she touched it. She looked for the footprints of whatever animal must have dug at the earth, a stray dog, perhaps, or, she thrilled to think it possible, a bobcat or a cougar. But instead of prints she saw a broad, flat piece of branch, fairly sharp on one end and blackened by dirt. She was puzzling over it when her father appeared above her, a piece of birch bark in his hand and the hint of a scowl on his face.

"What's this?" he asked.

Valerie shrugged. "Looks like someone was digging. But I've never seen anyone out here before."

"It was probably an animal. Coyote or something."

She shook her head. "Animals wouldn't put the dirt back in the hole."

"What about a turtle? Don't they lay eggs in holes then cover them up?"

"Not in the fall. And turtles use their feet to dig. But someone used a stick to dig this hole."

At the silence that followed her comment, Valerie looked up. She did not like the way the man was looking at her.

"Come on," he said. "Let's get your weeds and get back to the house."

They returned to the teasel patch where the man, wielding the birch bark like a potholder, gripped the stiff brown stems and sawed through them with his knife. He handed them to Valerie without looking at her. She arranged them with the other flowers, and then they walked toward the pines.

Valerie looked back to the spot where the disturbed ground lay silent at the foot of the great rock beyond the teasel, but at the man's stern glare she spun back and walked quickly to the edge of the ravine. He held his hand out for the flowers. Valerie gave them to him then scrambled down the roots to the creek bed below. The two of them followed the narrow path back through the woods, Valerie always in the lead, the man walking a few paces behind, bouquet swinging at his side. When they got to her grandmother's back yard, Valerie felt a hand on her shoulder.

"Here." He pushed the flowers toward her. "Why don't you give them to your mom."

She took the bouquet. "I think Mom might like getting flowers from you."

A sudden shadow flicked across his features, but he quickly replaced it with an impassive expression.

"Nah. I have to get going now. You give these to her. And, you know what? Why don't you just keep it to yourself that you ran into me out there. Your mother will just be angry at me for taking so long to get going to my new job. Let's make it our little secret, okay?"

Her brows knit in thought, Valerie stared at the flowers in her hands.

"Okay?" he prompted.

"Okay," she heard herself say.

The man looked at her a long moment. "Okay then. See you around." He melted back into the woods and she was left standing at the edge of the yard with a fistful of weeds.

Now, as wisps of gray clouds began to roll in from the west, Valerie stood on the edge of the snowy clearing and scanned the landscape until she spied the large granite boulder and several of the frosted dried flower heads of last year's teasel reaching far above the snow. Like flags indicating buried power lines, the spiky sentinels warned her to beware of what lay beneath.

With a queasy feeling growing in the pit of her stomach, she walked through the drifted snow to the spot. She pushed the snow aside with her right foot, then her left. She got down on her knees and shoved more snow back with her gloved hands, clawing at the ground until she could see the gray, frozen earth.

Grown over with grasses and wildflowers for many years, the ground was matted with dried vegetation and undoubtedly snaked through with fibrous roots. But she knew it could not be too far down. Not when the hole had been dug with a stick. She reached into the deep pocket of her winter coat and pulled out the folding metal camp shovel, then took aim at the hard ground and began to dig.

The only sound was the steady *shink shink shink* of the shovel cutting through dead foliage, like a distant woodpecker beating its head against hardwood. Minutes went by. She began to sweat with the effort. Finally she had to sit back a moment to take a breath and rest. She stared at the small indentation she had made in the earth after such effort and felt tears of frustration welling up behind her eyes. She fought them back, wishing she did not remember so clearly that the same emotions had come over her on that long ago autumn day.

Summoning as much anger as possible in order to tamp down the pain of abandonment, young Valerie had looked at the flowers in her hand. She walked back into the woods a few paces and set the bouquet down against a tree. She would not bring it to her mother. She would not let her grandmother know that she had ignored her warnings. She would not tell anyone about her father or the freshly dug ground. And she would not return to that part of the woods again.

That was the last time she saw her father but not the last time he crossed her mind. She thought about him the next day when the town was abuzz with the news. She thought of him as she read the articles in the paper about the search. She thought of him when another man was arrested. She thought of him when the suspect was released due to lack of sufficient evidence. Even as everyone else in town seemed to forget and move on as the case grew cold, she could not. And throughout her remaining years in that old white house, Valerie remembered that patch of teasel and the disturbed ground at the base of the boulder.

During college she was rarely back to visit for long, and once she had a career that involved frequent travel she had no time for ghosts. She wrote her grandmother letters on occasion, but she never went home. The look her father had given her that day by the boulder was blotted from her thoughts. The abandoned bouquet she had so carefully constructed ceased to enter her mind. Up until the day she got the phone call from her mother, she had been free of those grasping memories.

And now she was on her knees as the snow began to fall, chipping away at the frozen earth, looking for an answer she already knew in her heart. She pummeled and pried and scraped at the dirt, blowing away the snowflakes that had begun to accumulate in the hole. She removed her scarf and her wool coat, which now gathered snowflakes by her side. Her shoulders ached and her toes were growing numb. Just when she was about to give in to despair and sit back, defeated, she heard the unmistakable sound of metal hitting metal.

Valerie stopped. She pulled the shovel back and examined the hole. A sprinkling of rust mingled with the pristine snowflakes. A glance at the tip of the shovel showed the same. Hardly believing that there was truly something there, that the years of wondering were not merely a child's overactive imagination, she widened the hole, scraping away thin layers of soil like an archaeologist.

Minutes ticked by and the snow continued to fall from the ashen sky, but she doggedly pressed on until she managed to get the sharp tip of the shovel underneath the object and pry it out of its grave. She could feel her heart's relentless thump grow faster as she lifted the revolver up from the past into the cold light of day. Her hands shook as she turned it this way and that, then they fell to her lap, still clutching the rusty pistol.

Then the tears came. The tears that had never come to her before, that she had tried in vain to summon over the years when she thought about her father. They came now in a fluttering, gasping torrent. Not because he had never been there for her. Not because he'd left her on the edge of the woods that day. Not even because he almost certainly killed that man fifteen years ago. But because now she knew for sure that he had not been at the house to see her mother or to meet his daughter. He had been there to hide.

She sat back in the deepening snow and cried for what felt like a very long time. When her anguish was spent, Valerie was suddenly aware that she felt the cold deep within. Her body trembled now from the primeval physical desire to keep the organism alive. She looked around for her coat, shook the snow from it, and put it on. She snapped her scarf in the air and wrapped it around her neck. Ice cold drips of melting snowflakes trickled beneath her collar as she stood and stomped her numb feet. She had to get out of the woods.

Valerie looked at the gun. Should she bring it to the police and tell them about that golden autumn day? If her father was still alive, would this be enough to convict him? What of the victim's family? Didn't they deserve justice? But wouldn't they wonder why she had kept silent about her suspicions all these years? Could she withstand their confusion, their censure, their hatred?

The thought of being questioned by police and lawyers and reporters made her reel with lightheadedness. No, that was from too little food and too much physical exertion. She could not continue to stand there. She had to get out of the woods.

Valerie spun around on her heels and began to walk swiftly to the pines and the ravine beyond. Then she stopped. She could not bring the gun with her, its fate to be decided later. If she took it, she could not keep it. She would have to turn it in to the proper authorities. She could not simply stick it in a box and put it on a closet shelf, a macabre and twisted memento of the time she met her father.

She rushed back to the hole, placed the gun firmly in the space from which she had extracted it, and scraped the loose dirt over it. She stomped it down with her boots, smoothed away her footprints, and arranged the snow on top of it. It still looked suspicious, but the falling snow would cover her discovery. In fact, the snow had been covering all evidence of her expedition into the woods. If she did not hurry, she might lose her way back entirely. She would no longer have to worry about someone stumbling upon a forgotten murder weapon. They would be preoccupied with other matters when they found her frozen and lifeless body.

Valerie turned back to the pines and rushed into the trees without another backward glance. She skittered down into the ravine and trotted alongside the frozen trickle of water, eyes searching for the disturbance her feet would have made at her earlier descent. Because there had been no wind, and thus no drifting, she found the spot easily. It took a few attempts to scale the side of the ravine, but once she was back on level ground, she could still see the faint depressions in the snow where her feet had trod before. It was probably not the most direct route to her car, but she was not about to experiment with alternatives.

When she had entered the forest this cold January day, she had walked slowly, deliberately. Now she ran. And as she ran, the shaking subsided and the chill gave way to a warmth emanating from deep within her body. The trees filed by in quick succession, like telephone poles on a highway, and suddenly she was out.

She stopped at the edge of her grandmother's back yard, put her hands on her knees, and took a deep breath. Then she straightened and walked across the yard to her car. She got in, turned the key in the ignition, and put it in gear. Ten minutes later, Valerie was accelerating on the entrance ramp to I-96, putting a final distance between herself and her past, between that golden autumn day and this gray winter one. She fixed her eyes on the western horizon where the sun was just beginning to break through the clouds and gave a sigh of relief.

Then she remembered the shovel.

THE BEGINNING
AND THE END

The trip never should have happened—wouldn't have happened were it not for that unfortunate confluence of romantic clichés the night of Miles and Courtney's wedding. The twinkly lights of an outdoor reception under ivory tents. The warm honey glow of the dance floor. Romantic songs from a more romantic era. The lingering heat of an August evening that made everyone blush more freely, drink more deeply, flirt more openly. Men in tailored clothing. Women in strapless dresses. Shoes kicked from aching feet lying in haphazard heaps, leaning heavily into whatever other shoe happened to land nearby.

Nadine and Guy had met at the rehearsal dinner just the night before, but being the closest friends of the bride and groom, they already knew more about each other than most strangers. She knew he was a staffer for a state legislator, knew he went target shooting once a week, knew he was hoping to write a book. He knew she was studying to be a nutritionist but fancied herself an undiscovered singer, knew she loved the color turquoise, knew she was really a brunette beneath all that blonde.

When they found themselves entangled in an embrace, the last couple on the dance floor long after the bride and groom had left for their honeymoon, it seemed that their connection was deeper than a few hours of staring into one another's eyes might otherwise have produced. They had even already walked down the aisle of a flower-bedecked church, as if practicing for their own wedding.

"We should go to Paris," Nadine breathed into his ear as the strains of a vaguely French song died down. And with those five impulsive words, their course was set.

Guy snickered.

"No, really," she said, working hard to focus on his eyes. "We should go. You could write. I could find some little club to sing in. I could go by Nadia. It'd be divine."

Guy pushed away from her a little. "Paris?"

Nadine's lips curved in a wry smile. "Why not? I've always wanted to go to Paris, haven't you?"

Truthfully, Guy hadn't thought that deeply about international travel, but he certainly didn't want to close the door on spending a lot more time with the woman in his arms.

"Paris," he said.

"Let's do it," she said with more force. "Just for a month or two. If we don't do it while we're young, we never will."

So they agreed. But on Monday life began again. And Paris, though not forgotten, seemed to drift further from reach with each passing moment.

Nadine's summer tan began to fade. Guy put on a few new pounds around the middle as football season kicked off and many thousands of hot wings and beers were consumed. Classes were starting up and Nadine's parents flatly refused to continue to pay her tuition if she traipsed off to Paris with a man she had just met. Guy couldn't give up his position for anything less than a more advantageous one when there were so many young hopefuls waiting in the wings.

Shackled by reality, they settled for a weekend at a quaint bed and breakfast only a few hours north.

"We can take in the fall colors," Nadine suggested, though she had begun to resent the trees for how very common and American they all looked.

"But what would we do up there?" Guy wanted to know. "Isn't it pretty much just woods and farms Up North if you're not on a beach?"

"The website says this place has gourmet meals, beautiful grounds, lots of artwork on the walls."

"So we'll eat and walk around? All weekend?"

"No, you relax. Bring a book. They have chess and checkers and stuff." Nadine struggled to keep her voice positive.

Guy considered her very short list of diversions. "Is it near anywhere?"

"Of course it's near places. Everything is near something."

"So maybe we could go to some little touristy town Saturday and look around at least? I don't want to be stuck in some old house all weekend."

"Of course," Nadine assured him. "It'll be fun."

But Nadine had a little covey of doubts she had carefully tucked away in the back of her mind where they wouldn't make trouble. Was this too big a step for their very new relationship? Would he find her just as attractive as he had during the wedding reception when they had both had too much to drink? Was he really as appealing as she remembered?

On the last cloudy Friday in September, Guy found himself wondering why he was driving to Nadine's house to go spend a weekend with her. He hadn't seen her since the reception, had hardly even spoken to her on the phone, though they compulsively traded text messages. Still, it was too late to back out. The room had been reserved and the deposit had been made.

Le Petit Château billed itself as "a little taste of France close to home." When Guy and Nadine pulled up to the house, it did strike them both as appearing fairly French, though if Guy was honest with himself he knew next to nothing about architectural styles. For Nadine's part, she had thought it would be either a little more imposing and therefore exciting, or else a little more diminutive and therefore charming. Instead it was disconcertingly average.

The first sign of trouble ahead popped up behind the reception desk in the foyer when the smarmy desk clerk couldn't find their reservation. Guy was secretly relieved at this—he could lament it outwardly, curse their bad luck, then return home and get back to life as usual—but the reservation was finally found and the key handed over. The clerk took Guy's credit card, Nadine took the key, and Guy took the bags.

With each step up the creaky staircase, the bags grew heavier. Nadine had some trouble getting the key into the lock and turning it the right way, but managed to open the door, which promptly slammed into the dresser. Nadine entered slowly. Behind her, Guy maneuvered the bags through the too-small space and dumped them on the bed. The only bed.

"I thought we reserved a room with two double beds," he said.

Nadine looked at the bed as though she had never seen one before.

"I'll call the reception desk and tell them there's been a mistake," Guy said as he tried to read Nadine's reaction to the situation.

A short perusal of the cramped room revealed no phone.

"Be right back," Guy said. "Don't get too comfortable. I'm sure we'll be moving in a minute."

He scuttled downstairs intent on salvaging the situation. Not that he would mind sharing a bed with a beautiful woman—which Nadine certainly was, even in the unforgiving light of day—but moving too fast was something he prided himself on never doing. That was how political hopefuls got themselves in hot water. He couldn't risk Nadine contacting the local news someday when he was campaigning for a senate seat to accuse him of taking advantage of her ten years before. No one cared about what he did with his time now, but the moment he put his hat in the ring and started asking for votes, enemies working to discredit him would start appearing everywhere. He had to be smart about this.

He stood at the front desk, his fingers lightly tapping the wooden surface. A minute went by. Another. Another. Finally the clerk breezed into the foyer.

"Oh, I'm sorry to keep you waiting, sir," he said with no trace of remorse. "How can I help you?"

"There's been a mix-up. We reserved a room with two double beds and the room you sent us to only has one bed."

The clerk pasted an expression on his face that hovered between concerned and skeptical.

"Let me see," he said. He tapped ferociously at his keyboard. "Nope, I have you down for a single queen size bed."

"Okay, well, that's not what we asked for."

"Were you the one who called and made the reservation?"

"No, my…friend did."

"Well, then, perhaps she asked for a single bed." The clerk waggled his eyebrows at him.

Guy let out a frustrated sigh. "Do you have a room with two beds?"

The clerk gave him a onceover, perhaps trying to discern what was wrong with him that he would want to avoid sleeping with the sexy blonde woman whose fingers had lightly touched his own as she took the key from his hand. He pounded the keyboard and studied the computer screen.

"I'm afraid they're all occupied. Perhaps you should count your blessings, young man." He waggled his eyebrows again and gave a little leer for good measure.

"Yeah, thanks," Guy said curtly, then he started back up the stairs. Was it possible, he wondered as he creaked his way to the second floor, that Nadine had requested one bed?

He stopped outside the closed door of the room and tried to mediate the argument between his cautious and careless sides. True, sometime in the future sharing a bed with Nadine could prove to have been a disastrous lapse in judgment. But what if they fell in love? Got married? Made a life together? Looked back on this mishap fondly as the time when they knew they were truly meant to be?

On the other side of the door Nadine wondered why Guy didn't want to sleep in the same bed. Did he think she was repulsive? Was he secretly gay? Or was it just a show to prove that he was a gentleman and had tried to make her more comfortable? She checked her hair in the bathroom mirror and patted her face with tissue to absorb the oily shine that had begun to show through her makeup. Maybe that was what he'd found such a turn-off. That girl at the makeup counter at the mall had insisted that was the right foundation for her skin type. Oh, she would be getting an earful the next time Nadine saw her.

The door creaked open and she quickly crumpled up the tissue and tossed it into the trash can.

"What'd they say?" she asked Guy as he slid into the room.

He shook his head. "No rooms available with two beds."

"Mmm," she replied.

"Are you sure you asked for a room with two beds?" he asked.

"Hmm? Oh, yeah. Positive."

Guy shook his head once more.

"Well, let's just make the best of it," Nadine said. "We won't have to worry about it until tonight. In the meantime, what shall we do first? We have a couple hours before dinner."

It had started to rain outside, so they walked around the house and examined the artwork in the hallways. Neither was an expert, but you didn't have to be in order to see that there was nothing impressive here. When they had come to the last painting in the place—in a frightfully short span of time—neither could bring to mind clearly enough any of the works they had just seen in order to have a discussion about them. It was still an hour and a half before dinner.

A game of checkers with one piece missing filled twenty minutes. Solitaire filled the rest of the time, with Guy in a wingback chair hunched over the coffee table in the parlor and Nadine at an antique writing desk by the window so she could keep an eye on the rain.

They were called to the dining room by a gong and took their places on either side of a small table covered with a white tablecloth. Salt and pepper shakers in the shape of the Eiffel Tower and a little sign that said "Bon Appétit" in a scripty font sat next to a bud vase with a single yellow rose already tinged with brown. French café music was piped in from somewhere above on tinny speakers.

The food was good, though not good enough to warrant much discussion. As Guy and Nadine lifted forkfuls of duck to their mouths and sipped on a passable red wine, each searched for something to say.

"I've never had duck."

"Me neither."

The clinking of silverware against plates. Metallic accordion singing from the ceiling.

Guy took a deep breath and let it out slowly. "Hope the rain lets up."

"Yeah."

More clinking. A burst of laughter from a couple at a nearby table.

The man and woman were old, perhaps in their eighties if the wrinkles and liver spots and slow, deliberate, and somewhat shaky movements were any indication. Their eyes threw sparkles across the table to one another, which were caught and absorbed and thrown back. The decades they had shared as husband and wife were a sweet mystery, kept secret from others by the shorthand they had developed over a lifetime. A glowing orb of light surrounded them and kept their happiness bouncing between just the two of them, though trickles of laughter snuck out here and there.

Nadine sat back against the wrought iron chair and felt cold and dark in comparison. She had wanted to recapture the feeling of Courtney's wedding reception, where everything had felt bathed in golden light. There had been so much potential wrapped up in that evening. She looked across the table to Guy and tried to picture him as a wobbly old man with a skinny neck and large round glasses. But he was too handsome to get old. And she certainly didn't want to think about what she would look like in her eighties.

Guy kept his eyes moving about the room, flitting here and there from knick-knack to knick-knack. He didn't want to see the old couple's joy. He didn't want to see Nadine's conjured optimism. He didn't want to see the bones on his plate, scraped of flesh, sitting atop a sheen of grease. He felt the first petulant gurglings of an upset stomach coming on.

They powered through a rich dessert and sipped dark roast coffee, Nadine surreptitiously watching the old couple almost the entire time, Guy reading work emails on his smart phone under the table and trying to ignore the growing queasiness within his gut. The rain continued to fall steadily on the patio bricks outside. The sky slowly darkened. Then the plates and cups were empty and there was nothing to do but go back upstairs to that single queen bed.

Guy stood.

"You go on ahead," Nadine said. "I'll be up in a few. Think I'll have just one more cup of coffee."

"Sure, no problem." Guy was fiercely relieved that he would have some time to himself in the bathroom—if he could lurch his way up the stairs in time.

Nadine watched him go then motioned to the waiter for another refill. She turned her attention back to the old couple. Their mirth had dissipated and the bright light around them had dimmed slightly. Eyes once crinkled at the corners were now looking out from beneath concerned brows. She strained to hear the conversation but could only catch a word here and there. Were they talking about an ill friend? A wayward grandchild?

The waiter came by with the coffeepot and, noticing the direction of her gaze, became her informant.

"Those two have come here on their anniversary every year for the past fifteen years."

"Oh," Nadine said, "I wonder how long they have been married."

"I think it's sixty-four this year," the waiter said.

She looked up at him. "Sixty-four years."

"Yeah, though they say they've really been sweet on each other for a lot longer than that. Met in Paris during the war but couldn't get married until they got back to the States."

"I can hardly imagine that."

"Crazy, isn't it?" And with that he hustled back to the kitchen.

Nadine watched the ancient lovers. Their tender gazes seemed so natural, so unpracticed. Was there ever a time when that woman had looked at him and analyzed every minute detail of his expression, trying to discern his thoughts so that she could adjust what she was saying to get that expression to change? Had she ever taken it upon herself to attempt to move their relationship along, to get him to touch her, to love her, to commit to her? Had she ever asked for one bed at a hotel?

Looking at them now, Nadine was sure this woman hadn't resorted to such maneuverings. Love was supposed to come naturally. It grew by itself wherever it wanted and could not be eradicated by circumstance. Love was not like that browning yellow rose in the vase before her, forced into bloom in the wrong season, already decaying before it was even completely open. Love was dandelions.

Upstairs Guy sat on the bed with his head between his knees. Much of his dinner—he hoped all of it—had been flushed down the toilet. He had forced open the tiny bathroom window and shut the bathroom door in an attempt to hide his problem from Nadine when she finally came up from the dining room.

Just the thought of her drinking coffee down there, watching that happy old couple made his stomach queasy again. She wanted to get married to someone. He'd seen it on women's faces before. He wanted to get married too. But not to her. He could already tell it just wasn't right. They could never be that old couple.

He stared at the carpet and felt the four walls of the tiny bedroom pull in a little closer. He had no intention of letting things go any farther with Nadine, but he also had no plan, no way out. All he wanted was to be back home in his own apartment, getting sick on his own toilet, with no one around trying to pretend that nothing was happening on the other side of that bathroom door.

Guy heard the floor creak out in the hallway and tried to look interested in a magazine that had been left on the nightstand. A minute went by. Perhaps the sound had been his imagination.

Finally the door slowly opened and Nadine closed it quietly behind her. "Hey," she said softly.

Guy looked up at her as if he was just now noticing she was there. "Hey."

"So, I decided to call a cab to take me home."

"What?"

"I already paid the bill downstairs. You stay here tonight. I just think maybe we're pushing this a little. Too fast, you know?"

Guy felt simultaneously relieved and rejected.

"I'm really sorry," she went on. "I just...I just don't think we're...you know?"

Guy looked at her blankly.

"You know. It's just not happening for us."

Her expression told him that she was confident she had adequately explained her reasoning. She took a step toward the bed to gather her purse and her overnight bag, which had never even been unpacked.

"Well, can't I just drive us both home?" Guy offered. He couldn't imagine being trapped in a car for three hours bouncing down patched-up asphalt roads, stomach churning like a shaken-up two-liter. But a taxi service? The cost would be outrageous.

"No, no," she answered quickly. "It's already on its way. I figured we had to pay for the room no matter what, so someone should enjoy it. Anyway, you can have breakfast here tomorrow morning. The chef is apparently making frittata and homemade cinnamon rolls. Should be good."

At Guy's painful expression she rushed on. "I'm so, so sorry, Guy."

But it was simply the mention of food that had caused him to flinch.

"No, Nadine, it's fine," he assured her. "It's fine. I just...I wish it had worked out." Guy was surprised to realize it was true. He did want to be that old man someday, and it would have been nice to have found his old woman that weekend. And yet, Nadine wasn't her.

"Yeah," she said. "Listen, I'm going to head down to the lobby to wait for the cab."

"Want me to come wait with you?"

"No. No need. I'll be fine."

She turned toward the door.

"Nadine," Guy said. "Sorry about Paris."

"Don't be," she said with a little shake of her head and the ghost of a smile upon her lips. "It's still out there."

She walked out the door and Guy could hear her progress as the creaks faded away. He laid back on the bed, fished a book out of the side compartment of his overnight bag, and opened it where he had last left off. And at some point he realized that he no longer felt sick.

WE SHALL SOMETIME
COME TO SOMEPLACE

When Ted left the house that morning, the breeze carried memories of winter. He had donned a warm coat, thrown a box of catalogs into the back seat of his tan 1977 Dodge Charger, and set out for towns along M-46 that he hadn't yet hit. The temperature rose steadily as he drank his gas station coffee and stopped in to schmooze the owners of a few hardware stores, hoping to get them to buy what he was peddling. Though it was only March, towering cumulus clouds studded the western sky as if it were midsummer. And by the time he found himself on an empty stretch of highway around three o'clock, he had shed his coat, loosened his tie, and rolled down the windows to let the outside in.

It was then that the radio went out.

Ted twiddled the knobs. He rolled up the window. Rolled it down again. Static. With a frustrated sigh he clicked it off and looked ahead with confusion at the clear eastern sky. He focused on a bridge in the far distance, then a farm, then he glanced into the rearview mirror and felt prickles of panic at the back of his neck. The sky behind him was a flat, gunmetal gray.

He considered his agenda, his catalogs, his anticipated cash flow for the next month. Then he pressed on the gas and searched for a cross street that might tell him of his progress. Heedless of the new crop of potholes that had grown over the winter, Ted barreled down the highway, listening to the hum of road seams retreating beneath his tires, intent on checking another town off his list. If he could outrun the storm and make a couple more sales, he could probably cover rent with enough left over for beers with the guys on Friday night.

With a violent jolt, the front passenger wheel plunged into a deep gash in the concrete. The rusted-out front axel snapped. Ted's chin connected with the steering wheel as the car spun a bit then shuddered to a stop in the stubble of last year's corn.

Ted tried to curse, but the movement of his jaw sent a sharp protest of pain through his face and down his neck. He tasted metal. Pain coiled around his back. He killed the engine and swung the car door open with a creak. He twisted gingerly in his seat, stepped out, and walked around to the passenger side. He bent to get a look at the wheel, which was sticking out at an odd angle. The motion sent him stumbling onto the gravel shoulder and then into the road as the throbbing in his jaw exploded. With a firm hand on the hood of the car he stopped himself from falling over.

The storm front was moving quickly and Ted knew he would be in the midst of a hard rain within minutes. He fumbled at his pockets, searching for his phone, but they were empty save his wallet and yesterday's losing lottery ticket. Hadn't he had it earlier? He walked back around to the driver's side and lowered himself to the seat. Wincing, he reached around the floor of the car, looked into the back seat, dug in the box of catalogs. No phone.

He retraced his steps, tried to bring to mind the meetings he'd already weathered that day. Yes. There it was. Sitting on the lunch counter at that diner in Howard City. He looked up at the sky through the car window and then to the horizon, hoping to see the far edge of the storm, to see how long the rain might last. But the western sky was that same deep, hard gray as far as he could see. He examined the landscape around him. Just fields bordered by trees. The bridge. The farm. A drainage ditch that stretched perpendicular to the road into the middle distance and entered a large concrete pipe under a culvert.

The car seemed his best bet. He pulled his legs in, shut the door, rolled up the windows, and settled in as comfortably as he could. The rain couldn't last forever. Someone would drive by. Someone would see him. Let him use their phone or give him a ride to the next town.

Within a few minutes the first drops began to fall, sing-songy, on the roof of the car. The tempo and volume increased quickly and steadily as the sky overhead blackened. Inside the cab it got darker and darker until it was like twilight. Then Ted saw tiny white balls bouncing off the hood in front of him. He turned on his hazards and craned his sore neck to the southwest. And he knew that staying in the car was the wrong choice.

An angry cloud seemed to be stretching its fist toward the earth, slowly circling, grasping, clutching. Ted sat mesmerized a moment. Then a finger began to emerge from the fist and Ted searched frantically for the door handle. He burst from the car with no thought to the hail or the wind or his aching jaw and scanned the fields. Where was the bridge? The farm? So far away that in the black of the storm he could no longer make them out.

But there was the ditch.

Ted plunged into the hollow. Hands above his head to ward off the relentless hailstones, he ran as fast as he dared across the uneven, soggy bottom of the ditch. Just above the edge of the ditch, he could see that menacing finger reaching for a spot on the ground. He picked up speed, tripped, recovered, then tripped again, landing face first in the muddy water. The culvert beckoned just twenty yards away.

Stumbling onward, chest thrumming, adrenaline coursing through his body, Ted hurtled toward the culvert. He looked once more at the finger of cloud, saw it make contact and begin writing in the dirt, then dropped to his hands and knees at the mouth of the pipe. He crawled to what looked like the midway point of the murky tunnel, as far away from either entrance as possible, maneuvered himself into a sitting position, and braced his hands and feet on the concrete arching overhead.

As the wind roared past the mouths of the pipe, Ted realized with a little start of terror that he was not alone. Just a couple feet from him in his dim burrow, a soaked and stunned brown rabbit hunched transfixed. He tentatively reached out a hand toward the creature. When it didn't move, he placed his hand on its wet back. If it were possible, the rabbit flattened itself even more to the pipe. Rivulets of water rushed around it and its nose hovered a breath away from the stream.

Ted reached over its back, cupped his fingers beneath it, and in one swift motion pulled it onto his chest and pinned it there with a firm hand. It didn't struggle or squirm, just stared unseeing with glassy black eyes. Slender whiskers brushed Ted's aching jaw.

All at once the roar increased to a deafening, echoing mass of angry sound swirling through the pipe. Ted wanted to cover his ears. Instead he braced himself with one hand and covered the rabbit's ears with the other, as though somehow that gesture might win him some protection for himself. The finger of cloud seemed to probe the pipe, picking at its contents, trying to draw them out. It reached and scratched and raged. And just when Ted was sure he could not grip the inside of the pipe any longer, it gave up, moved on. The roar dissipated. The rain came in torrents. And then the wicked, twisting cloud was no longer his most pressing problem.

The rain was coming so swiftly the just-thawed ground could not soak it up. It flowed into the ditch and under the culvert and into Ted's lap. Still gripping the rabbit, he edged slowly out to the far end of the pipe and peeked at the sky. Hunching over to shield the creature from the worst of the rain, he crept out and poked his head over the edge of the ditch. A long black gash cut through the field. Far off in the other direction, the funnel cloud zagged its way northeast. It was moving on and he needed to as well.

He scrambled out of the ditch, walked a few steps, and set the rabbit down on the sodden ground. When it didn't move, he clapped his hands near its face. He nudged it gently with his foot, but it sat unblinking in the pouring rain.

Though he was sure it was unwise, he tucked the rabbit under his arm like a football, then started back toward the road and his car. But then, where was his car? He scanned the road in the distance and saw no tan 1977 Dodge Charger. He looked over the surrounding fields but could not see anything resembling a car. Then, as though dropping from the clouds, colorful pieces of paper floated down around him. He bent to pick one up and the blood pooled in his head and the throbbing began again. He straightened, waited for the sparkles in his vision to clear, and then focused on the paper in his hand.

His catalogs.

With a sense of astonished euphoria at having survived, Ted slowly followed the ditch back to the road where his car had been. He stood in the rain staring at the spot and had a sudden sinking feeling in his gut. He had been in that very place just minutes before the tornado must have wrenched the car from the earth and deposited it who knew where. And now he was holding a wet rabbit on an empty road.

He turned right and walked toward the bridge he knew was there, not bothering anymore to shield himself from the rain. Every inch of him was wet through anyway. After what seemed a very long time, he reached the bridge and stood in its shelter. He put the rabbit down at his feet and together they waited.

The temperature plummeted. The wind whistled across his soaked clothes. He was shivering violently. Recalling the farm, Ted climbed up the side of the embankment to the road above and looked south. In the gloom he could just make out the shapes of a large farmhouse, a barn, and two crumbling silos. He poked his head back down to check on the rabbit. It had not moved. He picked up his fellow survivor and the two of them headed for the farmhouse.

With each step it seemed the rain let up a little bit, the sky began to lighten, and soon Ted could see the house clearly. It seemed no more hospitable than the culvert had been. The once white paint was dirty and patches of bare wood siding showed through here and there. The roof showcased two different styles of shingles along with some sheet metal. The yard was peppered with rusted-out farm machinery.

Approaching the porch, Ted hesitated, wondering if the crooked planks could take his weight. They groaned in surprise as he made his way to the front door. Seeing no doorbell, he knocked firmly on the door and waited. After a moment he balled his fingers into a fist and pounded hard with the side of his hand. Nothing. He tried the knob and when it yielded to him he felt a mixture of relief and trepidation.

The door creaked into the black space and Ted took a faltering step.

"Hello?"

Then stronger. "Hello?"

He could only hear rain.

The room was a bit untidy, but not enough to suggest abandonment. Ted walked down the short hall, poking his head into a half bath, a kitchen. Then he looked up the staircase and said again in a loud voice, "Hello?"

Hand on the rail, Ted began slowly climbing the stairs.

"Hello, young man," came a gravelly voice from behind him.

Ted whirled and nearly lost his footing. Involuntarily he clenched his fingers around the rabbit and it writhed in sudden fear, then leapt from Ted's hand. It shot down the stairs and disappeared under the couch in the front room.

An old man stood near the foot of the stairs.

"I'm sorry, sir, you startled me!" he said in a rush. "I was caught in the storm and I saw your house and I thought perhaps you might have a phone I could use. The tornado took my car."

The old man nodded. "I see. I was down in the basement. Heard you come in, but it took me a minute to get up the stairs. Legs aren't what they used to be."

Ted descended the steps and held out his hand to the old man.

"I'm Theodore Gale."

The old man stretched out boney fingers. "Peter."

"Well, Peter, I'd be very grateful if I could make a call."

"Of course, boy. Follow me into the kitchen."

Peter walked smoothly down the hall on silent feet, almost floating. When he passed a wall sconce his shadow was thrown upon the opposite wall and seemed to be disconnected from the man. In the kitchen Peter motioned toward the phone on the wall. Ted picked up the receiver and held it to his ear.

Silence. He hung it up and tried again, but there was no dial tone.

"Looks like your phone is out, sir," he said to Peter, who stood by Ted's shoulder with a small towel in hand. Ted took the towel, carefully wiped his face, then dabbed at his dripping hair.

"Eh? That so?" Peter said flatly. "Doesn't surprise me."

Ted thought for a moment.

"I don't suppose you might be able to drive me to the nearest town?"

The corners of Peter's mouth inched down. "I would if I could, boy, but I haven't driven in years."

"You don't have a car, though?"

"'Fraid not."

Ted frowned.

"Only thing I think I can do for you right now is let you get dried off so you don't freeze."

With no other option before him, Ted accepted the offer. The two men walked back toward the staircase and there in the living room, snuggled between two lumpy pillows on the couch, was the brown rabbit.

"Oh! I'm sorry," said Ted as he made a move for the animal. "I completely forgot. This is—"

"I know what it is," Peter said gravely as he waved his hand. "No explanation necessary. Come follow me upstairs and we'll get you settled."

"Okay, I'll just see if I can put it outside," Ted continued.

"No, no. Just leave it alone. It'll be fine there for now."

Ted stopped his forward motion and locked eyes with the rabbit, who, it seemed, truly saw him for the first time now that it was not in a state of terrified shock. It looked at the same time tame and wild, friendly yet aloof. And, Ted noted with some measure of confusion, it seemed to know something he was not privy to.

He shook off this strange thought and caught up to Peter, who had by this time ascended the stairs. Peter removed a couple towels from a hall closet and then led Ted into a spare bedroom.

"There are some clothes in the closet there. Help yourself. There's no dryer here, but you can hang your wet things over the shower curtain and put your shoes on the heating vent. Once you're dressed, come on down to the kitchen and I'll get you something warm to drink."

At the click of the closing door, Ted hesitated but a moment and then commenced stripping down to his underwear. He rubbed his bare skin vigorously until he was dry and warmth began to creep back into his feet and hands. Then he stood before the open closet and considered his options. A few minutes later, clothed in a plaid flannel shirt and too-big jeans cinched at the waist with his own wet belt, Ted crept down the stairs. He avoided eye contact with the rabbit stretched out on the couch.

Peter wasn't in the kitchen as he said he would be, but the hissing and gurgling of the coffee pot told Ted his warm drink was on the way. He sat at the table and waited. He examined the repeating pattern of the wallpaper until he discovered grotesque faces in the flowers and flourishes. He deliberated about the flooring, finally deciding it was linoleum. He picked at a crack in the veneer on the edge of the table. Finally Ted got up and walked to the window.

Peter was not outside. He walked to the top of the basement stairs.

"Peter?" he said loudly to the dark chasm below.

When no one answered, Ted trotted down the stairs and flicked on the light switch, fearing he would be greeted with the sight of Peter's crumpled body at the foot of the steps. But the only thing he saw was tidy shelves lined with canned goods. He searched the house, every room, calling out to his host. Met with silence everywhere, he went back out the front door, the rabbit's black eyes following him, and headed for the barn across the street.

The rain had ended but the sky remained clouded and dark, and Ted wondered what time it was. He scuffed across the gravel drive and came to the barn. The sliding door stuck and he had to put his shoulder into it to get it to budge. As he squinted into the dim structure he knew immediately that Peter could not be in the barn. There was hardly room for a mouse to scamper through the accumulation of junk that obscured every inch of the dirt floor. Furniture, tools, discarded children's toys, smashed baskets, moth-eaten quilts, and what looked like the bones of some unfortunate animal lay in haphazard arrangements throughout the large, musty space. It looked like a place dreams went to die. A shiver crept up Ted's spine as he backed out and shut the door.

Back in the empty house, he began to wonder if he had imagined the old man. With no other options, he returned to the kitchen, checked the phone for a dial tone once more, and poured himself a cup of coffee. He walked into the living room, half expecting the brown rabbit to have disappeared like the old man, but he spied it under the coffee table snuffling along the rug. A short search in the refrigerator revealed a bag of carrots. Ted slid one from the bag, got down on his hands and knees, and poked the carrot out in front of him as an offering.

The rabbit sniffed the air and regarded him with an appraising look. It scooted back a few inches and hunched down. Ted left the carrot on the floor and sat in a nearby wingback chair. From that vantage point he couldn't see the creature, but eventually he did hear crunching. Above the rabbit on the coffee table a chess board was set, Indians on one side, pirates on the other. Ted fingered the carved feather headdress of the king and wished very much that Peter would come back to play.

Minute by minute the light in the house dimmed and failed and darkness crept in. Ted didn't know how long he had been in that chair or what time it was when he suddenly came to, but he did know that he needed a bed. Leaving the rabbit to its own devices, he walked up the stairs and once more checked each room for Peter. Once more he came up empty. He laid down on the bed in the spare bedroom and, though troubled by thoughts of his missing host, soon succumbed to a deep sleep.

When he descended the stairs the next morning in the weak light of a cloudy dawn, Ted saw the rabbit sitting on the front mat and staring at the door. He didn't want to let it out—they had been through quite an ordeal together—but of course he knew a wild rabbit could not stay in the house. And, in fact, he could not stay in the house either. It wasn't his house, and he really ought to call the police to report the old man's disappearance. With some measure of sadness, he opened the door and the rabbit, without a glance back, hopped out onto the porch. Ted closed the door and went for the phone again, just in case. He did not expect a dial tone and did not hear one. So he pulled on his shoes and went out onto the porch himself.

The rabbit was still on the front step, sitting on its haunches and scanning his surroundings. Ted adopted a similar pose and searched in vain for another house on the horizon. There was nothing. Nothing but sickly yellow fields and the road that stretched in both directions. Finally he turned toward the highway where he had come the day before. He would stand out on the highway, wait for someone to pass by, and catch a ride to the nearest town to report all that had befallen him and get some help. But after hours of standing, pacing, sitting, then standing again, not one car had passed.

In the early afternoon, Ted gave up and returned to the house. He passed the rabbit foraging for clover by the porch, intent on finding sustenance of his own. Bologna on white bread chased with a glass of water recharged him somewhat, and he set off again, this time in the other direction, determined to walk until he found another house. He walked for hours but saw nothing besides blackbirds and a flock of geese flying in formation. Fields of stubble stretched on and on, divided by occasional lines of still bare trees. Quick rests on a stump or a rock on the side of the road became longer and longer. As the sun skulked behind the clouds and day took on an evening hue, Ted had to decide whether to press on and risk being stranded outside overnight or to turn back. One thought of the tornado he had narrowly escaped had him turning on his heels and doggedly striding back to the house.

This same pattern was repeated the next day and the next. Ted succumbed to a few moments of near hysteria at the thought that he was trapped in the middle of nowhere, in a place with no border, a vast, stretching, senseless emptiness that he knew, in his more rational moments, just simply could not be. No farm was this remote. There must be neighbors. But he could never reach them. Never walk fast enough and far enough before night drove him back.

He soon decided he needed to prepare for a longer trip. Packing food would be easy—crackers, cans of beans, tuna fish—but finding shelter would not. After much searching, Ted found an old blue tarp. Patched with duct tape and fitted with a few cross-country skiing poles he had discovered in the recesses of the basement, the tarp would make a decent tent. Every evening he would plan for his hike, tell himself that tomorrow was the day. But when morning came it seemed too daunting. Too far. Too difficult. And he stayed where he was.

Days began to run one into the next with no sense of time. Ted ate little, worried more about the finite store of canned goods he'd discovered in the basement than what might have happened to the old man, whom he'd practically forgotten. He felt himself growing thinner, moving slower, sleeping longer. He noticed gray hairs in the mirror as he washed up at night. His stubble slowly expanded until a salt and pepper beard covered his cheeks and chin. He hardly recognized his reflection. He chalked it up to extreme stress and tried to avoid mirrors, eventually taking them off the walls and storing them face down in the basement.

And each day, or nearly so, he saw the brown rabbit. It lolled around the yard, darted in and out of bushes, slept in sunbeams on the front porch. At Ted's slow approach it would squat down in that way rabbits do, thinking they cannot be seen. But if he reached out a hand to touch it, the rabbit disappeared in a flash of white tail.

Then all at once, Ted felt himself give up. One morning he lingered over coffee and corned beef hash in the kitchen. Instead of lacing his shoes up and hiking down the street, he walked barefoot out onto the porch and sat on the step. He watched the rabbit over the edge of his cup as it nibbled at a weed on the far side of the road a few yards from the barn.

The sound started so low and distant that Ted wasn't aware of any change in the air until the car was in view far down the road. When he spotted it, his heart jumped a bit in his chest, but he didn't know why. He was sure this meant something—but what? As it neared the house, the car slowed and from the corner of his eye Ted saw the rabbit disappear through a hole in the side of the barn.

The car rolled to a stop in front of the house and the driver slowly cranked the window down and leaned out. She was young, blonde, and wore a hopeful expression.

"Excuse me, sir, I hate to bother you, but I'm wondering if you know how I could get to Freeland. I went wrong somewhere and I need to get back on track."

Ted wrinkled his brow. "Hmmm...Well, it's been a while now since I've been on the road, but..." He looked up and down the long, straight expanse of asphalt. "I suppose if I was you, I'd get back on M-46 and head east a ways. Maybe that's your first step, uh..."

"Alison," the young woman supplied.

"Yes, that's what I would do, Alice." He nodded his head vigorously to confirm his shaky advice.

She smiled. "It's Alison. Anyway, thank you, sir. I'll be on my way. It looks like it may rain and I'm late."

She rolled up the window and proceeded down the road. Ted watched the car get smaller and smaller until it merged with the gray clouds on the distant horizon. When it was gone, he turned to watch the rabbit again. But it was in the barn.

ONE ENDLESS SUMMER DAY

I gaze through last year's dirt on my mother's kitchen window. It is closed despite the heat, painted shut at some unknown date before my birth, but I'm so distracted that this previously obvious fact escapes me. I need more air than the oscillating fan in the corner offers, so I unlock the window and strain to lift it until memory looks at me and says in a matter-of-fact tone, "Well, what did you expect?"

The small square of yard complains of neglect. Overgrown grass shimmers in the languid breeze. Along the rusted chain link fence stand the stoic remains of a few forgotten rosebushes, misplaced impatiens burnt from too much sun, prickly weeds growing undisturbed wherever bare dirt had shown through in the spring. All unwanted reminders of my parents' advancing years.

Even through the shut window I can hear the metallic tinkling of the mobiles and wind chimes my stepfather has made out of cans he could not repurpose down in the basement workshop, but also could not bring himself to throw away. A sparrow lands briefly on what was once an empty milk jug, now a birdbath. She tilts her head to examine it. Dry. She pants a moment, beak agape, then flies off in search of a more hospitable yard. About the only thing thriving in this oven of a city are the dandelions.

I knew instinctively when I woke this morning that it would be a long, tiresome day bookended by several hours in the car in heavy traffic. I tried to appropriate some of my daughter's zeal for highway gridlock and the prospect of a day at Grandma's, but it wasn't easy to summon much enthusiasm.

We arrived at ten o'clock amid smiles and hugs and bouncing childish steps. The shock of exiting the air conditioned sterility of the car and stepping into thick, sluggish summer nearly choked me. But Karen seemed wholly unperturbed by the heat and headed off for the garage to search for the cat that hated her. I followed my mother up the porch steps. After a quick hello to my stepfather and some perfunctory small talk about the heat, my mother quickly launched into what I knew would be her primary activity for the day.

I sat across from her at the kitchen table and began the dance. I nodded in agreement, raised my eyebrows, pursed my lips, and shook my head at appropriate times. After awhile I furtively checked my watch then walked to the back window where I am now as she continues to talk.

I am about to resume my place at the kitchen table when a small girl in a yellow sundress prances through the back gate. At five years old, Karen is still enraptured by life. No small thing escapes her notice. No feather is left unexamined in the grass. No flower is left unstudied. No creeping or flying creature is ignored. All are catalogued, processed, made valuable in the noticing.

I watch her tip-toe along the brick-edged garden beds, undoubtedly noting their colors, shapes, scents, and textures. Her legs and arms are tan, her hair a few shades lighter than normal, her bare feet brown from accumulated miles of summer dirt.

"Paula, would you be a dear and feed the cat while you're up?"

The only reason this registers in my brain is because it is a direct request. It stands out in sharp contrast to the barrage of passive aggressive complaints I've been enduring for forty-five minutes. My sister has not paid back a loan, yet she and her husband went on a cruise. The neighbors have been on vacation and did not hire someone to keep their lawn mowed. The car is making a funny noise and she had hoped my husband would have come to visit with me so he could take a look at it. Countless other grievances about doctors, grocers, hairdressers, the postman—every conceivable person who is not her.

As I reach for the cupboard that has always housed the towering stacks of cat food cans, I wonder what she says about me to others when they are conscripted as listeners.

"No, use the one from the fridge."

I open the refrigerator and am immediately assaulted by the acrid, vaguely meat-like smell of an open can of cat food. She's left the thin curved circle of aluminum on top, but bits of the noxious mixture glisten on the lip of the can. I lift it gingerly with my fingertips, retrieve the cat's bowl—the same empty margarine dish for thirty years and four cats—and paw through the silverware drawer for a dessert fork.

The sound of scraping is all it takes to draw the cat to the kitchen from wherever it has been skulking. It slithers provocatively around my ankles and looks up at me with an expression that wavers between gratitude and disgust. When I put the bowl on the floor the cat stares at it a moment, looks up at me, and says, "This isn't what I ordered."

I leave him to his disappointment and return to my mother's.

The woman has been complaining, as far as I can tell, for thirty-seven years, though I suspect that it has been going on for much longer. Evidence to support this theory: my stepfather's tendency to avoid talking to her at all cost; her excessive skill, suggesting a lifetime of practice; and my own desire to believe that it was not my birth that got her started in the first place.

She strings her sighs and frowns like beads upon a thread, a master artisan working skillfully in her chosen medium. I imagine that she has been making this necklace of criticism and slowly winding it around my neck for decades, the weight increasing with each year. Some day it will choke me entirely. One cannot have a mother like mine and not feel in some uneasy way that one is in grave danger of turning into her.

I become aware of a low grumbling undercurrent like distant thunder, different in tone from her crackly voice. I look out the window at what I am sure was a cloudless blue sky just moments ago. The bright sky blinks back at me. Then I hear the sound again. It's coming from inside the house.

My stepfather's deep snore mingles with the sounds of a motorcycle race on the old tube TV. I can make out the ghostly shapes of dirt bikes through the clouds of dust kicked up by the racers and the TV static. The video tape is probably twenty years old. The picture has warbled and fuzzed in the same spots since I was a teenager when my stepfather first proudly pushed the tape into the VCR and adjusted the antenna to get the clearest possible picture, which of course was not clear at all.

I think of the static of my own hazy childhood days. I know something dreadful must have happened, but I can't put my finger on any precise memory. My father's drinking, his affairs, his cancer, the way he kicked me when I hid under the bed. His death, perhaps. There must have been something that created the woman before me. But no amount of squinting through the erratic black and white snow can bring it into focus. Instead of trying to reclaim my own vanished youth, I turn halfway in my chair to look out the window at youth in full bloom.

My daughter crisscrosses the yard, hunched and seeking, plucking buttery yellow dandelions from rosettes of jagged leaves. She picks one, squeezes the white fluid to the end of the stem, and sticks out her tongue. She draws back and grimaces at the bitter taste then tosses the flattened dandelion aside and resumes her quest for more. The bouquet in her hand expands until it is an orb of soft sunbeams.

"Paula, could you warm up my tea?"

In the other room, my stepfather has abruptly come back to life.

I retrieve the cool mug from his rough hands, place it in the microwave, and turn the dial. It whirs to life, rattles the mug, turns it slowly. *Ding*. The mug burns my fingers, but the tea is still lukewarm. One more time. *Ding*. Steaming.

I bring the cup back into the front room and place it upon my stepfather's collection of water stains on the end table.

"Careful. It's hot."

"Well, that was the point."

He smiles at me and for that moment I forget my mother's monologue of discontent.

As I walk back to the kitchen, a flash of yellow through the window catches my eye. The bouquet of dandelions has been entrusted to the vigilant eyes of an old stone rabbit sitting on its haunches in the garden. While he watches over the flowers, Karen spins in ever-widening manic circles, the skirt of her dress ballooning, her tan arms outstretched. She tumbles to the grass and her shrieking giggle breaks through the windowpane. She rolls onto her back and spreads her arms out, palms down, fingers gripping the grass to reacquaint herself with solid ground as she stares up into the blue sky.

I remember that feeling.

I stand at the counter fiddling with an ice cube tray longer than necessary so I can keep my attention on this precious girl. On her stomach now with her chin on the ground and the lawn up to her eyes, she is singularly focused upon a blade of grass in front of her. I lean closer to the window and squint to see. Then she pokes a finger up to her face and there upon her fingertip is a speck of red. Blood? No. She is smiling.

A ladybug.

The insect marches down her finger and hand and partway up her arm before it stops, braces itself, then opens its fancy carapace and lifts off. I follow its zig-zagging flight into the blue sky and imagine going with it. The sound of my mother prattling on and on melts away from my consciousness. The buzzing of motorcycles becomes the hum of the ladybug's wings and I ride upon its back, spinning in the air, looking down on the yellow girl who is up and spinning again too.

"Well?"

The sharp edge of my mother's voice wrenches me back into reality and I am pulled back from the bright green, blue, and yellow world outside, sucked back into the musty house and the faint smell of cat food emanating from the margarine dish.

"What?"

"Haven't you been listening to me?"

I struggle to find an answer as I fill my glass with water from the sink. My mother sighs for the seven hundredth time this day. I sit back down across the table.

"When do you think Dan can get down here and tar the cracks in the driveway?"

"I don't know, Mom."

I don't tell her that he could have come today, but preferred to spend his day off on more enjoyable pursuits.

She drones on and I cradle my chin in my hand, trying to focus on her eyes behind her thick, bifocal lenses. They are pale blue marbles set in skim milk. Puffy half-moon sacks hang like hammocks below, then mottled skin draped over unremarkable cheek-bones. Jowls drawn into a permanent frown frame crooked lips painted the wrong shade. Her sagging countenance pulls me down, down, down with its terrible gravity.

Is that how I will look when I'm old?

I attempt to appear attentive and yet steal looks into the back yard. My daughter cartwheels, somersaults, walks on her hands, repeats. Then she must notice her reflection in the very window through which I am watching her, because she marches right up to it and begins making faces at herself. When her repertoire is exhausted, she backs up and begins to dance to some tune in her head, jerking and shaking this way and that, assessing every move in her reflection. I watch her from my secret spot with a sad smile on my face.

When did she get so big? It seems to have happened when I wasn't looking, perhaps one night as I was sleeping. It vexes me that time will soon steal away her abandon, that most precious of childhood qualities. To be unconcerned, flitting about on the very edge of reality in the silvery world of forests and fairies, wearing a dress made of yellow rose petals and riding upon the backs of ladybugs. To lightly touch down upon the ground on soft bare feet. To wear necklaces of raindrops. To talk to fireflies.

"Paula, what are you looking at out there?"

"Karen. Just watching Karen play in the yard. I'm listening. You were talking about the prices at the meat market."

"It's really just ridiculous, you know. I've never paid so much for ground chuck in my life."

And on and on and on. The whining motorcycles from the front room. The buzzing negativity from across the table. I squeeze my eyes shut and push my fingers into my temples.

"Mom, do you have any aspirin?"

"It's in the bathroom."

I go into the bathroom, shut the door, and stand for a moment in the lovely still dark, my hands upon the counter. Then I flick on the light and open the medicine cabinet. I scan the jars and bottles lined up in rows, a neat little train of powdered normalcy that daily delivers some relief, some steadiness, one more miserable day upon this earth to the two old people who live in this sad little house.

I tell myself that I need to be more patient with her. That life has not always been kind to her. That I'll be old someday. That she just wants someone to talk to.

I wrench the top from a bottle of aspirin, swallow two pills with water from a paper cup, and turn off the light. I linger at the bathroom door and spy the cat watching me from my stepfather's lap. He is asleep again. The cat dismisses me with a turn of his head. Then the back door creaks open and the cat bolts for cover under the couch.

A quick pattering of bare feet across the linoleum. I look around the corner and see my daughter skipping in, her hands obscured by the massive dandelion bouquet.

"Grandma, I picked these pretty flowers for you! Look!"

She thrusts them at my mother, who does not leave her spot at the table.

"Oh, Karen, those aren't flowers. They're just weeds. Dandelions are weeds. No one wants those."

The look that crosses my daughter's once happy face causes the bubble of irritation that has been slowly building within me all day to burst into sudden hot anger.

"Mom, she's just trying to be nice. What the hell is wrong with you?"

I push my rage into the kitchen and bang around in the cupboards until I find a vase. I fill it with water and gently take the dandelions from Karen's hands. I put the bouquet in the center of the kitchen table, blocking my mother's face from my daughter's view, then take her hand and lead her out the back door and into the yard. I swing open the hot metal gate and we walk down the weedy driveway to the shaded front porch.

I sit down on the top step and pull my little girl onto my lap.

"Have you ever heard the story of the witch and the weeds?" I ask.

She shakes her head mournfully.

"Once upon a time, in a land not far from here, there was a girl who loved life," I began. "She had a nice family and a beautiful garden she loved to spend time in. Then one day she grew up and she forgot how to love life. She stopped seeing the good in things and started looking for the bad. She looked at her garden, which had once been her greatest joy, and saw only work that needed to be done. Raking and digging and planting and watering—things she had always loved to do—became odious tasks."

"What does odious mean?" she interrupts.

"It means something you don't like to do at all."

She nods and waits for me to continue.

"Well, one day the woman, whose bad thoughts by that time had turned her into a witch, got so fed up with the garden that she cursed it and abandoned it. She went off to live in a cave and grew older and sadder and crookeder. In her garden the beautiful plants began to die with no one to care for them. They withered and dried in the hot sun. Thorns and ragged prickly plants began to take over the roses and peonies and lilacs. Weeds."

My daughter looks very concerned about all this.

"But," I continue in a brighter tone, "when she cursed the garden she forgot to say the very end of the curse, which would have completed the spell. So today even weeds that no one wants in their garden have pretty flowers, and the most beautiful of all the flowers that most people call weeds today are dandelions. Their lovely round faces are bright yellow to remind us of the sun. Not everyone can see their beauty. Only the very young and the very smart."

"What happened to the old witch?"

I lay my cheek on her warm hair.

"She still lives in her dark cave. But from time to time she sees a bit of sunny yellow out of the corner of her eye, waving in the breeze outside the entrance to the cave."

"The dandelions?"

"Yes. They're beckoning her, calling her to come out and love life and care for the garden and laugh and dance around like she used to."

Karen twists around in my lap and looks me in the eye. "Will she ever come out?"

"Someday, I think she will."

It is a lie, but a child's story must always end in hope.

Her wounds now forgotten, my daughter trips away toward her secret chamber beneath the huge spruce tree and I face the prospect of visiting the witch in her cave a little longer. I check my watch and die a little when I see it is still not quite twelve o'clock.

Back inside the house my mother is making sandwiches for lunch. We do not speak of the dandelions. There is nothing to say. There have been many times I have wanted to ask my mother why. Why can't you just smile and say thank you when your granddaughter brings you a gift? Why don't you just stop loaning money to Jackie? Why can't you just be happy? But asking why is fruitless. Every why voiced is merely another opportunity for my mother to cry woe is me.

Lunch passes without incident. Grandpa regales Karen with animal tales while my mother and I chew in silence. Soon my stepfather reclaims his recliner and flicks the TV back on and my daughter takes off for more adventures outside.

The afternoon crawls. The house gets hotter and hotter. Sweat trickles down my back. No amount of ice water and iced tea can offer relief. From time to time the back door creaks open as Karen comes in to share a discovery. When she opens her hands to reveal a grouchy brown toad, my mother cautions her, "Don't let the cat get at it." When she solemnly bears a robin's broken eggshell to my side, my mother says, "That's filthy. Take it out of this house." When she comes with news of the delicious cookies the neighbor lady has given her, Mom warns, "Better watch yourself, Karen. You don't want to get fat."

Finally I call Karen inside out of the sun. Even as tan as she is, there's still the danger of sunburn or heat stroke. She pretends to play Solitaire on the floor in front of the fan.

"You're doing that wrong."

"Mom, she's five."

She pretends to be a kitty and jumps up on Grandpa's lap to be pet.

"He never gets out of that chair," says my mother from the chair she has occupied for hours.

Finally my watch tells me I have done my time and I am free to go.

"You're not leaving already?"

"Yes, we have to get on the road. I want to beat the traffic."

"It's too late for that. You might as well stay a couple more hours and leave after rush hour."

"No, I think we need to get going. Thanks for lunch."

We say our goodbyes, make our escape.

I feel my muscles relax as I pull onto the expressway between two semi trucks. Every spin of the tires propels me further from what I fear to become.

"Mom, look!" Karen exclaims from the back seat.

"I'm driving. I can't look."

"But look! There's a ladybug on your shoulder!"

I glance. A ladybug marches over the relaxed contour of my shoulder.

"Can she come home with us?"

"I think we better pull over and let her out."

Karen is disappointed.

"What if she gets lost in the car by the time we get home and we can't let her out?" I reason. "We wouldn't want her to starve."

Karen gasps. "Let's let her out."

I pull onto the next exit ramp and stop the car along the side of the road.

"Stay here and don't unbuckle your seatbelt."

I walk a few steps onto the weedy roadside and coax the little red insect onto my finger. When I hold it up toward the sky it lifts off and in a moment it is gone.

Back in the car I give my daughter a smile. "I think she'll be very happy out there."

As fields and houses and barns fly by, the horizon ahead beckons me home.

"Mom," my daughter says sleepily from the backseat, "this was the best day I think."

"Really?" I say, not quite believing I heard her right. "The best one?"

"Yeah, so far."

I try to imagine the day from her perspective. I reach my hand to the back seat and feel her soft little hands wrap themselves around mine.

"You may be right, sweetie."

WATER & LIGHT

Ava Kimball hurried as quickly as she dared across the icy parking lot, squinting against the snow and the strands of hair that lashed at her eyes. The cold cut through the black coat she had long since been unable to zip up and she gripped the collar together in one clenched fist, her large belly protruding like a nervous actor parting the curtain to watch the audience file into the theatre.

Winter had finally made its entrance this Christmas Eve and snow now plummeted to the ground at an incredible rate. This was decidedly inconvenient for anyone traveling for the holidays but especially so for Ava. Just a week from her due date, Ava was tired, cumbersome, and resentful of the call that came a half hour before, asking her to fill in on the night shift. She knew it only amounted to sitting in a chair for nine hours and watching dials shiver, but at this point sitting for any length of time was uncomfortable.

As the flags in front of the nondescript gray building snapped wildly, Ava fumbled for her keys, her hands cramped from the bitter cold. She wrenched the heavy glass door open and shouldered her way in right before a gust slammed it shut behind her. The sound ricocheted in the stark lobby. Ava shook the snow from her hair and stomped her boots on the mat, then gingerly stepped onto the tiled floor, squeaking her way to the stairs. It was only one flight up, but with the baby in her womb taking up most of the space her lungs used to occupy, one flight of stairs now felt like ten. She pushed the elevator button and waited.

When the doors didn't open immediately, she knew that Ross must have taken the elevator when his shift started earlier that day. Ross, who was young and not pregnant, but was arrestingly lazy.

The doors opened.

"There you are, Ava," came Ross's exasperated voice from within the small box. "I was beginning to think you'd never get here."

Ava looked at her watch. "I'm two minutes early."

"Yeah, well, not by my clock."

"I just got the call like thirty minutes ago. I came as fast as I could."

They switched places and Ava held the elevator door open with her foot.

"So were you just going to leave before I even got here?"

Ross looked away to the right.

"No, I was just going to check the parking lot to see if you were here yet."

Ava took in Ross's heavy winter coat and wool hat. Keys jingled from his gloved hand.

"Whatever, Ross."

She pulled her foot into the elevator and the doors began to slide together.

"Merry Chris—"

The last part of Ross's perfunctory holiday greeting was muffled as the elevator rose to the next floor. Ava walked out and looked over the railing to the lobby below. But the only thing there was a small puddle of melted snow where she had been standing the moment before. Ross was probably already scraping his car windows in the parking lot.

She sighed heavily and lumbered to the control room.

Before she could even slip off her coat, a flashing red light on the panel caught her eye. Was that why Ross was so eager to be on his way? Had he pretended not to see it so he could pass off the inspection to her?

Over the past few months, Ava had gotten used to complete strangers fawning over her—pulling out chairs and opening doors and carrying groceries to her car—so Ross's utter disregard for her condition felt wholly inexplicable. At least Max had apologized profusely and promised future favors when he'd asked for her help covering his shift. And in his defense, she was probably the only employee who didn't have plans for Christmas.

Ava dropped her bag and gloves on a chair, scribbled some numbers and letters on a scrap of paper, and headed for the water conditioning basins. The moment she walked through the door she felt her blood pressure drop. The rhythmic sound of the water rushing into one basin, draining from another, then rushing in again filled her ears. Echoes of trickling water droplets sang to her from the far corners of the vaulted ceiling. Her own heart rate seemed to fall in sync and she nearly forgot about her inconsiderate coworker.

The immense room was edged in large pools of water in various stages of the softening process and bisected by a wide hall. Built at the height of the Art Deco era, the lines were clean, orderly, and geometric—squared pillars of concrete, circular lights and dials, aerodynamic chrome consoles that looked like they belonged on a sexy roadster rather than in an otherwise unassuming municipal building. Reaching out from the central hall and suspended over the basins were narrow walkways that provided access to valves and levers and buttons, all pieces of the intricate machine that drew water up from an aquifer deep underground, prepared it for use, then sent it careening through a vast network of pipes and into people's kitchens and bathrooms.

Ava turned and stepped down onto one of the walkways. When she reached the other side she scanned the controls on the wall. She adjusted the pressure on the offending pump, looked over the rest of the dials, and concluded that all was well.

It annoyed her that Ross couldn't be bothered to do such a simple task. The water treatment plant was old and required constant monitoring, but generally problems were small and easily fixed. Perhaps it was the ease of the job that had attracted Ross in the first place. For Ava it had been the promise of a steady paycheck and decent insurance in a town where many people didn't have either.

Problem solved, Ava turned slowly, her belly brushing the railing, and began to shuffle back to what she thought of as dry land. She took one step up to the main hall and felt a sharp pain in her abdomen. She sucked in a breath and let it out slowly. She'd gotten so used to aches and pains during her pregnancy that she thought little of it and continued back to the control room.

She tried to read, shifting around in her seat in a futile attempt to get comfortable. Every twenty minutes or so she despaired and stood up to walk around. The pain she'd felt earlier returned now and again, but no warning lights flashed on the control panel. Ava wished they would. Having a task to do might help take her mind off of her discomfort, which, she had to admit, was more than simply physical.

Unmarried and far from the family that raised her, Ava had been trying to convince herself for weeks that being alone this Christmas did not bother her. She didn't have to buy any presents or waste money on decorations. She'd been invited to a couple parties that hadn't been horrible. She would have liked to see her mother, but most airlines wouldn't let a pregnant woman fly so close to her due date and Mom was terrified of flying. Anyway, she was planning to drive in once the baby was born to help Ava around the house and meet her first and likely only grandchild. Ava certainly couldn't expect more than that.

Not long after the clock rolled past 11:00 PM, Ava pulled out a snack and brewed some coffee in the tiny break room. She had studiously avoided caffeine for most of her pregnancy, but she needed it this night.

As she stood at the counter, gripping the handle of the gurgling coffee pot, waiting for it to sputter to a stop, Ava felt a wetness below. There was no water on the counter in front of her and if there had been, she knew from experience now that her large stomach would have intercepted it before it got to her legs. She hadn't even been able to see her own thighs without a mirror for a month.

She reached down and touched the spot on her pants, which seemed to be growing. It was warm. Coffee? Then all at once it hit her.

She hobbled back to the control room and dug in her purse for her phone. When she found it, she hesitated. Who should she call? Max was out of town tending to his father in the hospital. Ross had surely turned his phone off to avoid calls from work now that he was free for the night. Her boss was in Florida for the week. She settled on calling her mother to tell her to start driving.

Never able to get any bars from deep within the concrete building, Ava carefully walked toward the elevator. She had to stop twice to put a hand against the wall and breathe through her pain, but managed to get herself down to the glass door to the parking lot. One bar appeared on the phone's display.

She dialed and waited. Then waited some more. On the fourth ring, a distant, sleepy voice crackled out, "Hello?"

"It's me. It's time. You need to get up here."

"It's time? Now?"

"Yes, now."

"On Christmas Eve?"

"Yes. It's Christmas Eve." Ava felt another pain coming on.

There was the sound of muffled movement on the other end of the line.

"Ava, it's nearly midnight! I can't leave now. I've barely slept and the weather guy said Michigan was having a terrible snowstorm. You know I can't drive in snow."

Ava suppressed a scream and said in a measured tone, "Fine then. Get some more sleep and let the salt trucks make the rounds, but please come as soon as you can in the morning." She felt tears coming on. "I can't do this alone."

A beat of silence.

"Ava, you know that was your choice."

"Don't, Mom. Not now."

Her mother sighed.

"I'll be there as soon as I can tomorrow. I'll call when I leave."

"Mom?" Ava gritted her teeth as a wave of pain passed over her.

"What?"

"I'm at work and I don't know what to do."

"You're at work? Why are you at work?"

"Someone called in because his father went into the hospital with a stroke or something and I was the only one with no Christmas plans. And now I don't know what to do. I can't just leave."

"Ava, you're having a baby. I don't think they'll fire you over that."

"I know, but what if something happens?"

"What could happen? Ava, you need to get yourself to the hospital."

"I don't think I should drive."

"No, you shouldn't. Call an ambulance."

"Isn't that expensive?"

"You have insurance, right?"

"Yes, but—" She was cut off by another contraction. "Oh, Mom, I don't know. These contractions are coming pretty fast."

"Don't worry, honey. First babies never come fast. You have plenty of time. Now stop talking to me and call an ambulance. I'll see you as soon as I can get there tomorrow."

"Okay," Ava said meekly. She would be a mother in a matter of hours, but she had never felt so like a scared child than she did at that moment. It took three tries to get her shaky fingers to punch 911 correctly on the touchscreen, but then she froze a moment, her thumb hovering above the send button. Was having a baby an emergency? Wasn't it pretty common? Perhaps she should call information first and get the number to the hospital.

Another wave of pain and she clenched the phone in her hand. A moment later a she heard a voice.

"911, what's your emergency?"

Ava explained her situation to the dispatcher, who said they would send an EMT out to the water treatment plant but that it might take a while because of the weather. The plant was outside of town and the first priority that night was the many car accidents on the increasingly treacherous roads and highways.

"Do you want to stay on the line with me, ma'am?"

"No," Ava said. "I'm sure you'll have your work cut out for you with the weather. I'll be fine here. I can wait."

"Are you sure?"

"Yes, I'm sure."

"Then I'll call you back to check on you in about an hour if the EMT isn't there yet, okay?"

An hour? Ava hissed out a breath as another contraction subsided.

"Okay, thank you."

"Don't worry, ma'am. Women have been having babies for thousands of years and the first one always takes longer than you think."

She shuffled back to the elevator, leaving behind a puddle of fluid. Her pants were now soaked. She knew about water breaking, of course, but in all of her preparatory reading she had never realized that once it started it occurred with regularity, just like the water gushing into the conditioning basins, ever refreshing itself after it drained away. Only this wasn't soothing at all.

Ava went back up to the break room. She turned off the coffee pot and poured its contents into the sink. She certainly didn't need caffeine to stay awake now. Every cell in her body seemed to vibrate with nervous energy. She slung a couple dishtowels over her shoulder and gathered two packages of rough brown paper towels in her arms, then hobbled out to the hall.

Back in the control room, Ava scanned the console for problems. The same light that had been on when she first got there was again blinking a painful red. She shoved a crumpled handful of paper towels into her pants and slowly headed once more to the cavernous conditioning room, stopping once along the way to breathe through a contraction.

She inched down that skinny walkway to the controls on the wall, leaning heavily on the rail during another spasm of pain, and made some more adjustments on the malfunctioning pump. Then all at once the room went black. The perpetual background noise of humming ceased and all Ava could hear were the mingled echoes of dripping water and her own surprised gasp. Then the generators kicked on.

Emergency lights illuminated the room in an unfamiliar way and the productive hum of pumps and fans ramped back up. Ava could see her way back to dry land, but strange shadows teased her as she moved back to the control room. Once there, she refreshed her paper towels, put on her coat and gloves, and reached for a flashlight. A contraction welled up inside of her and she gripped the desktop and the back of her chair as the pain gradually drained away.

Flashlight in hand, Ava went back to the elevator. She was about to get in when she imagined the power going out again, perhaps for good this time. She opted for the stairs, gripping the railing and taking each step as though the staircase were made of ice. Three steps down she was forced to stop as another contraction hit.

Finally safe on lobby level, she dragged the floor mat to the door and pushed hard against the glass. Snow was already piling up outside the door despite the salt on the concrete. Ava had to push hard to get it open, then she wedged the mat in the doorjamb to keep the door from shutting and locking her out.

A frenzy of white snow reflected the meager glow from the porch light. It was powered by the same generator that now kept the water moving through the pipes, but the parking lot beyond was dark. Ava turned on the flashlight and started a slow circuit of the building. Her wet pants froze to her legs within seconds.

Around the corner she came upon a large tree which had evidently toppled under the weight of the snow and the fury of the wind. It now rested on a set of power lines. Ava put her hands on her knees and breathed through another wave of pain then stood as straight as she could. With nothing to be done about the tree, she turned back and fought her way against the wind to the propped door. Snow had already blown through the opening and into the lobby. Ava struggled to drag the wet mat back in and shut the door against the weather. She shook the snow from her coat and hair and took a long look at the stairs.

Before tackling the steps and finding some way to warm up her frozen legs, Ava quickly called in the outage. The woman on the other line told her she certainly wasn't alone. The power was out on a number of grids.

But Ava was alone—utterly alone—at that moment. The generators might keep the lights on and the water moving, but where was the EMT? Where was her mother?

When she hung up the phone another contraction built up and as it reached the top of the curve it pushed out the tears she had been holding back. Then her phone rang.

"Hello?" she managed.

"Ms. Kimball?"

"Yes?"

"Hi ma'am, it's Mary with the 911 dispatch. How are you holding up?"

Ava couldn't keep the anxiety from her voice as she said, "Okay."

"The ambulance is just a few miles away, ma'am."

"Okay."

"It's been slow going with the weather and there are a lot of traffic signals out. They have to take it slower than they'd like to."

"I understand."

"How far apart are your contractions, ma'am?"

"I don't know. Pretty fast, I think."

"Try to start timing. The EMTs will want to know that."

"Okay."

Another contraction.

"Ma'am, are you still there?"

Ava nodded and clenched her teeth.

"Ma'am."

"Yeah," she managed.

"Ma'am, are you able to get somewhere comfortable and lie down?"

"I'm in the lobby. Our power went out. I was just checking on it. A tree is on the lines."

"You don't have power?"

"No, but there are generators. But I'm in the lobby and there are stairs to get back up to the break room. There's a couch there."

"There's no elevator?"

"I'm a little afraid to get in it. What if it gets stuck? Anyway, the door is locked and the EMT would have no way in if I'm not here."

Another contraction.

"Can you prop the door and take the stairs—carefully—back to where you can lie down?"

There was a pause as Ava breathed through the pain.

"I think so."

"Okay, why don't you do that. The ambulance is close, but from the sound of your voice and the state of the roads, there's a chance you'll be having this baby there—with their help, of course."

Ava let out a whimper.

"It'll be okay, ma'am."

"Okay."

"Why don't you prop that door now and get yourself somewhere comfortable."

Ava hung up and did as instructed, once more wedging the mat in the doorjamb. Snow blew in through the cracked door behind her as she slowly scaled the stairs, stopping twice this time for contractions. At the top her heart was racing. After two more contractions she was finally at the control room. The red light was blinking insistently. Ava wavered. She needed to lie down. But the light continued to blink. And she didn't want to leave it to chance.

She took a slow, deep breath and took the everlengthening walk back to the water conditioning room. At the outside wall upon the narrow walkway, she tried to focus on the gauges but her head swam. She made some adjustments to that finicky pump and then slowly sank to the concrete floor in pain and near exhaustion. When it finally came time to push this baby out, would she even be able to?

She pulled out her phone. There were no bars, of course, but she could check the time. 1:47 AM. She should be asleep right now. In her mind she cursed Max's father for the lifetime of poor health choices that likely landed him in the hospital. She cursed Max for taking the easy way out by calling her, knowing she would need the extra pay to cover some of the expenses she would soon incur. She cursed Ross for his laziness. She cursed her boss for having enough money for a vacation someplace warm. She cursed her mother's timidity. She cursed this baby's absent father and then cursed herself for sending him away without even sharing the knowledge that he had fathered a child.

There on the hard gray floor, Ava sat in an ever-widening puddle of amniotic fluid and wept. The sound bounced around the vast empty room, clashing with the steady drone of the machines and the full, round tones of rushing water.

***

The voice was distant at first. Ava hardly realized she'd heard it until it grew louder and more insistent. But then, there it was—clear, calling to her.

"Ava?"

She stopped crying and held her breath.

"Ava Kimball?"

"Yes," she whispered.

"Ava?"

"Yes!" she shouted this time, then the shout became a moan as the pain hit her again. "I'm in here!"

The door at the end of the hall opened wide and a man in white rushed in.

"Ava?"

"Here," she said in relief.

He jogged down the narrow walkway and knelt in the dark half circle of fluid at her feet.

"Oh, thank God," she said.

"Don't worry. I'm here. Let's get you off this floor and to somewhere a little better suited to having a baby, shall we?"

He stepped over her limp body and braced his back against the wall, then he hunched down and stuck his arms under hers.

"Ready? One, two, three!"

Ava stood with a groan then nearly collapsed. She didn't know how long she'd been sitting on the cold, hard floor, but her legs felt like jelly.

"Whoa!" said the man in white. "Come on. Slow and steady."

Together they shuffled down the aisle to the step up to the main hall, pausing twice for contractions. After another count of three, the man hoisted Ava up the step and they began a slow, stilted walk toward the door, her right arm slung over his shoulders. Ava wondered why he hadn't brought a gurney.

"Will we be able to get to the hospital?" she asked.

He looked apologetic and shook his head. "I'm afraid not. You're going to have this baby here."

A contraction wracked her body and they stopped walking.

"Do you have anything with you for the pain?" she asked when she could speak again.

He shook his head again and opened his mouth to speak.

"I mean," she interrupted, "I know I can't expect an epidural or anything, but do you have any Demerol or something?"

Another contraction and Ava's legs gave out entirely. She squeezed her eyes shut against the pain as the man lowered her safely to the floor.

"Well, maybe we will have to do this right here," he said.

When Ava opened her eyes she could see the man had a couple white sheets and several white towels. She hadn't remembered seeing anything in his hands when he first burst through the door. The man gently helped her take off her boots and the wet pants that wanted to cling to her legs. He tucked a couple towels under her elbows and draped a sheet over her lap for modesty's sake.

Ava let out a guttural moan as a tsunami of pain crashed into her, nearly taking the breath from her lungs.

"This baby is going to come any minute, Ava," the man said as he knelt between her legs.

"Have you ever—"

More pain. Ava's moaning echoed all around her.

"—done this before?" she managed to finish.

The man smiled reassuringly. "I've been there for countless births, Ava. Do not be afraid."

He hadn't quite answered her question the way she'd been hoping, but with the burning pain she was now feeling between her legs she was suddenly past caring. This child had to come out. Now.

With a few agonizing pushes and a sustained groan from Ava, the baby finally broke free from her body and the pain quickly lessened. The angry cries of new life came on the tail of that last echoing groan and the sharp sound almost hurt Ava's ears.

"You have a son, Ava."

She let out a sigh of relief and lay all the way down on the cool floor which felt good against her sweating back and neck.

The man wrapped the child in a clean cloth and laid him on Ava's deflated stomach, then turned his attention to the afterbirth. Another push and Ava's womb was empty. With effort, she lifted her head to gaze at the wailing child in her arms. His eyes were clamped shut and he was covered in the fluid that had helped sustain him as his little body had been knit together in the dark places. Ava let out a little laugh then looked for the eyes of the man in white who had delivered her.

He was not there at her feet as he had been a moment ago. She turned her head in every direction, eyes searching the strange shadows cast by the e-mergency lights. But the room was as empty as her womb now was.

Then the door at the end of the vast room opened wide and two men in blue uniforms rushed in, pushing a gurney.

"Ma'am, we got here as fast as we could," said one as he knelt down beside her and began looking over the baby. The other quickly checked her vitals and then lowered the gurney to the floor.

"I guess you got on pretty good without us," the first one said, smiling at her. "Let's get you two cleaned up. Hold on to that little one."

The men lifted Ava and her son onto the gurney and covered them both up with a clean sheet. As they wheeled her toward the door she looked back at the spot on the floor where she had just been. Her pants and boots sat in a small, lumpy pile beside a dishtowel soaking in a dark stain of blood. The sheets and fluffy towels the man in white had used to comfort and cover her were gone.

She looked back to the baby in her arms. The boy was wrapped tightly in a second dishtowel.

"Where is the man in white?" she asked the EMTs.

"Not sure who you mean, ma'am," one of them replied.

"The one who delivered this baby. He was here right before you came in."

The men exchanged a glance.

"Don't worry ma'am. Everything is going to be okay."

They pushed the gurney through the door, down the hall, and into the break room. Clamps and scissors. Soap and water. Towels and blankets. And finally they were ready to transport Ava and the new life in her arms to the hospital.

Before the gurney was wheeled out of the break room, Ava glanced at the schedule on the wall and was pleased to see that the next name on the lined paper was Ross's. In a matter of hours, he would be stepping through the glass door and making the rounds through the building. He would be the one to clean the floor in the conditioning room.

The EMTs took Ava and the baby down to the lobby. Then one rushed out to ready the ambulance, backing it up as closely as possible to the door to assure that the new baby and his exhausted mother would not be exposed to the cold any longer than necessary. Ava covered her baby's face lightly with the blanket and pulled her wool coat up to the top of his head.

"Ready?" the EMT asked.

Her phone rang from inside the coat.

"Can I see who that is?"

"Sure."

She pulled the phone out and answered it.

"Hello?"

"Honey, I'm just calling to tell you I'm on my way."

"Okay, Mom. We'll see you soon. Drive careful."

"Everything okay?"

Ava looked out the door to the flashing red lights bouncing off the snow.

"Yeah, everything's fine."

She hung up and gave the EMT a nod.

Within seconds she was in the ambulance and they were moving slowly off the curb.

"Hey," the EMT in the back with her suddenly said with a smile, "Merry Christmas."

"Merry Christmas."

DRIVE

The business I'm in is run on trust. Or it was. Now we've got deposits and fines and all, but mostly we still have to trust that when someone rents a Haul-It truck to move their stuff from point A to point B, that we'll get the truck back on the day we all agreed on, or close to it. Most of the time it works out just fine. But once in a while, we have to go get a truck that never made it home. Maybe it was abandoned in a grocery store parking lot or on the side of the road. I've seen them in some strange places—and some in places I didn't care to go.

Back in early October I got a lead on the first truck we ever lost. Some smarmy realtor walking a property up near Houghton in the Upper Peninsula called and said there was a Haul-It truck back in the woods a ways that looked like it'd been there for years. Once he gave me the license plate number and I did a little detective work, I found out that it had. Twenty-five years, in fact. It was that very truck that made the boss raise the security deposit and add the fines and eventually start using GPS tracking.

Realtor wanted it out of there, of course, and even though the boss had written it off and collected the insurance money long ago, the thought of getting back the first truck he ever lost made him half wild. So I told him I'd come up and tow it back home and see if we could salvage it. Figured a drive Up North that time of year would be a hell of a lot nicer than hanging around the store anyway. Seemed like all I saw was the gray guts of that little rental office for days at a time.

I started out early morning on the twenty-third of October. Plopped my tired butt in the tow truck, got some coffee at the gas station, and settled in for a long drive. I turned the radio on for some noise— tape player's been busted for years—and pointed myself north on US-127 for a two-day trip.

As the miles ticked by I thought about that first lost truck. Boss didn't have much of a fleet back then. Called the police and filed a report, but they never found anything. He was raging around for weeks, threatening all sorts of violence if he ever laid eyes on the guy again. All I remember about the guy who rented it was his pitch black hair and pale blue eyes with dark circles under them. Creepy looking guy.

I must have been fresh out of high school then. Thought it would be a summer job while I figured out what I wanted to do with my life. Twenty-five years later and there I was going to get that very truck. I don't think that guy was even moving to the UP. Seems to me it was Flint or something. Sometimes I thought maybe he'd just gone to Canada and not looked back. Definitely wasn't copper country. I still remember those eyes.

I made it to the bridge before lunch, loaded up on fries and Coke at the last McDonald's for hours, and headed for the interior on the longest, straightest, boringest stretch of highway in the state. That far north the leaves were past peak already and the trees are kind of scraggly anyway until you get to the lake, so there wasn't much to look at. I kept turning the radio dial for something worth listening to. Eventually I just turned it off and listened to the road. Seemed like I was driving forever. I finally got to Houghton when the sun was going down. I found my motel, laid back with a pizza and a six-pack and the remote control, and forgot all about that truck and those pale blue eyes 'til morning.

When I woke up it took me a minute to remember where I was and why I was there. I felt like I'd been dead and was just struggling back to life, that pizza still sitting in my gut and my head throbbing from too much beer and not enough sleep. After some black coffee, I took out the little scrap of paper I had with the directions on it from the realtor and got back up in the tow truck. Time to go get that Haul-It truck and beat it if I was going to get home in time to watch the Lions.

The actual address wasn't all that hard to find, but finding the truck was near impossible since the realtor didn't bother to note the GPS coordinates. I was slogging through mud and pushing through briars and tripping over roots for a good hour, getting angrier and angrier at that stupid realtor and his stupid directions, before I finally stumbled on the thing by pure luck. For just a minute I was relieved. Then I realized with a sinking feeling that I would need more than a tow truck to get that thing out of the woods.

Of the twenty-five years it had been missing it must have been sitting right in that very spot the whole time judging by the size of the trees all around it. Maybe when that pale-eyed man drove it in there it was nothing but a few saplings, but now the thing was hemmed in on all sides by trees that would have to be chopped down before it could ever be dragged out. If I could even get the tow truck back here in the first place. Whatever dirt road might have been there all those years back was completely overgrown now so that you'd never know there had ever been even a footpath. I cursed that realtor out loud. He could've told me to bring a chainsaw, the idiot.

One thing was sure. I wasn't getting back for no Lions game.

I pulled out my phone to give that realtor a piece of my mind and to ask him if there was some way to get the tow truck back there, but since I was out in the middle of nowhere I couldn't get a signal. I cursed again. If nothing else, I could get a closer look and see if it was even worth trying to retrieve the truck or if a quarter century in the woods had reduced it to nothing but a pile of rusty metal. If it was completely trashed, I could just leave it and that idiot realtor could find some other schmuck to remove it because I sure as hell wasn't going to do it.

I walked up to the rear of the truck and along the passenger side. The tires were flat and it looked like it was up to the axles in mud. What looked like poison ivy grew up over the trailer and wound around the broken side mirror and up the bent radio antenna. I couldn't see anything through the filthy window so I yanked at the door, but it was stuck. The windshield was cracked and the cab looked like rusty Swiss cheese. The hood was half-open and creaked loudly when I forced it the rest of the way. Looked like mice had been living in it for a while.

I came around to the driver side and saw basically the same thing. All signs pointed to a lost cause, which pleased me quite a bit. Sooner I could stumble my way back out of these woods the quicker I could get on the road. Boss wouldn't want this truck. It was as good as dead. Wasn't worth the extra gas it would take to drag it home.

I was about to start my hike out of the woods when I found myself wondering if anything had been left in the trailer. That happened sometimes. Normally it would just be a box of books or something and we'd slap a sticker on it, give them a call, and they'd come pick up whatever they'd left. Occasionally someone would lose an earring or bracelet or something and we'd put the stuff in a lost and found box and wait for them to call about it. Now, I was pretty sure we weren't going to be able to find the mysterious guy with the black hair and the pale blue eyes even if he had left something in the truck. But that was part of the draw. Anything I found, I could bring back to the boss as partial payment for his stolen property. And maybe it would keep this trip from being a complete waste of time. Maybe I wouldn't find anything besides a dead animal or two. But if I didn't look, I knew I'd always wonder.

I came around the back of the trailer, got a firm grip on the handle, and planted my feet. Then I yanked up as hard as I could. I nearly went flying as the door opened smoothly and easily, as though it had been cleaned and oiled the day before. Once I regained my balance, I leaned into the trailer.

It was dark inside. I pulled out the little flashlight on my keys, but that tiny bulb only lit up about a foot in front of me, so I climbed right in. The floor was surprisingly clean and it didn't smell like dead animals in there. It didn't smell great, but it could have been worse. I took one step forward and nearly tripped. I shined the light near my foot and saw what looked like the corner of a mattress. Seemed a strange thing to miss when unloading a truck, but maybe the thing had had bed bugs.

I shuffled along the floor a little further and swept the space with that dinky light. Fuzzy-looking blankets and a flattened pillow sat on the mattress in a heap. Next to the bed sat an old fashioned little gas light like the ones you see people carrying around in movies that take place in the 1800s or something. In the back corner was what looked like an old kerosene heater and then I realized that that was part of the smell in there. Sitting on top of the heater was a beat-up metal coffeepot and a blackened frying pan. A rickety looking table held some camping-style tableware and the chair tucked under it was draped with some sort of animal pelt.

"I'll be damned," I muttered to myself.

Someone was living in the back of that old truck. Where was he? Had he heard my loud approach and taken off? Had he seen the realtor walking the grounds earlier that month and moved out? If he was still living there, what would happen to him when that realtor managed to get someone to tow his house out of the woods?

I sat down on the back bumper of the truck and squinted out into the woods. Was someone out there watching me right that moment? Maybe he wouldn't show himself until the intruder in his home was gone. Or maybe he'd just shoot me dead before I even knew he was there.

I got up and decided that this wasn't my problem. I wasn't towing it home. Might as well get back on the road and let nature take its course.

No sooner had I turned around to shut the door than I heard a voice that sounded like it hadn't been used for quite some time.

"Can I help you, mister?"

I spun around and found myself looking straight into a set of sunken, pale blue eyes. The hair was longer, more gray now than black, and his face was covered in a thick pepper-gray beard, but I knew it was him. I'd never forget those eyes.

"You want this truck back, don't you?" he said.

I gathered my wits up off the ground and answered him like I had expected to run into this very situation from the get-go. "How'd you know I was here for the truck?"

"You're from Haul-It, right?"

I couldn't tear my gaze away from those eyes. "You remember me?"

"Course I remember you. You handed me the keys. It's hard to forget one of the last people you really looked in the eye. You're a little more filled out now than you were back then, but I guess you were just a kid."

I noticed then that he held two dead rabbits by the ears in one hand and a shotgun in the other.

"You haven't seen another person in twenty-five years?"

"Oh, I see people when I go into town for fuel or canned goods once in a while, but I don't really look at them. Mind my business, they mind theirs. They don't really see me anyway." He paused a moment. "You here for the truck, then?"

His face looked sad but resigned, like he'd known this day was coming. Only there was no way I was taking that truck back with me.

"No, sir," I said, eyeing that shotgun. "Was thinking about it, but I don't think we'll take it back. Looks like it's found a new life. Anyway, wouldn't probably be worth fixing."

"I did feel pretty bad about not returning it," the man said.

"Don't you worry about it. Insurance and all, you know? Just got a call from someone about finding it out here in the woods and we had to follow up."

The man looked at his battered boots and nodded. I don't think I ever felt so bad for another human being as I did in that moment.

"Have you really been living in this truck for the past twenty-five years?"

He nodded. "Yeah."

"None of my business, but why? I mean, isn't it cold? What do you do all day?"

"Oh, I keep busy enough. In the spring and summer I gather berries and plants, in the fall I collect apples and nuts, in the winter I hunt and trap, and I fish all year long. I cook over an open fire outside most of the year. Heater keeps me warm in winter. I do all right."

"You know you're probably poisoning yourself with that heater in that small space."

"Nah, I got a little vent rigged up near the top of the trailer to let the fumes out."

I considered his situation. "What if you get sick?"

"I muddle along."

I thought of my TV and my phone and the mall and the movie theater and all the restaurants by my apartment. "Don't you get bored?"

"No, not really. I've got the sunrise and sunset and the stars. Sometimes I get to see the Northern Lights. I swim in the lake, watch the birds. Got a few books."

He must have noticed the skeptical look on my face because he went on.

"I don't miss anything, really. Well, maybe it would be nice to occasionally have someone to talk to. But I've had a couple dogs over the years, and that helped. Dogs are good company. You're their whole world and they notice if you're gone and come find you."

"What about a wife or a family or at least a woman now and then?"

His facial muscles tensed beneath that beard as he pursed his lips and shook his head.

"Nope."

I didn't believe him.

"Listen, I have to dress these rabbits. Why don't you sit down and take a load off. I'd offer you water but it would probably make you sick since you're not used to it straight from the stream. How about some coffee instead?"

"Yeah, all right."

He leaned the shotgun against the wall and handed me the coffeepot. He grabbed a large stockpot I hadn't noticed before and put a few other things into it. Then he headed off into the woods with long, sure strides. I trotted to keep up.

A moment or two later we came up to a metal grate standing in a pile of ash encircled by stones. He removed a can of instant coffee from the stockpot, along with two tin mugs, some dried plants, some roots, and a small knife.

"Could you fill this pot about three quarters full of water from the stream down there and the coffee pot too? I'll get the fire going."

I wandered off in the direction of the sound of running water. It took me a while to find the stream, then a while longer to find a way down, then a while more to dip the coffeepot full of water and pour it into the large stockpot about a hundred times. Lugging the full pot back up the incline and finding the campfire took a considerable while longer yet and I was sweating by the time I finally got there.

"Here," I said as I set the pot down on the ground. "I sure as hell hope that's enough because I'm not going back for more."

The man chuckled and looked in the pot. "That'll do."

In the time I was gone, he had built the fire and skinned the rabbits.

"What is all that stuff?" I asked, pointing at the dried plants and weird white roots that sat on the log next to him.

"Wild parsnips and some dried herbs."

"What are you making?"

"Rabbit stew."

I wrinkled my nose and thought of the hot wings I would not be eating in front of the Lions game tonight. Then I sat heavily on a stump. What was I doing out in the middle of nowhere with this mountain man?

Things were pretty quiet as I watched him boil the rabbits and cut up the roots and crumble the herbs into the pot. He stirred it with a big stick and pulled a bag of salt from his pocket and tossed some in. Meanwhile, he boiled up the water in the coffeepot and handed me a steaming cup. Then he sat on his haunches in front of me.

"So, what do you think of my simple life out here?" he asked me with a satisfied smile on his face. "Not too bad, eh?"

"I don't know," I said slowly. "It's all right. It does seem kind of...lazy."

His smile faltered. "Lazy?"

"Yeah...You don't have a job. All you must do is sleep and eat and sit around. I don't mean any offense and all, but it just seems kind of lazy."

I probably shouldn't have said it, but he didn't seem surprised by my answer.

"Okay, let me ask you something," he said, smiling again. "Why do you work for Haul-It?"

"So I can make a living?"

"You asking me?"

"No," I said. "I work there to make money to pay rent and buy food and go out for drinks with my friends. I work there because people need jobs."

"Do you enjoy yourself at work?"

"It's all right, I guess. Hours are a little long."

"If you didn't have to work in order to pay rent or eat, would you?"

I thought about that a minute. "No, I guess not."

"So if you could still live the way you do now without having to work, you wouldn't work."

I shrugged. "Nah, I guess not."

"Okay, then. Does that make you lazy?"

"But I *do* work."

"But you'd prefer not to."

"But I *do*. I'd rather buy food at the grocery store than skin my own rabbits and dig for roots. I like running water in my house. I work for that stuff. I pay for space I live in. I'm not squatting on someone else's land."

"No one was using this land. For twenty-five years no one has used it at all. Someone owns it I guess, but me living here hasn't hurt him or cost him anything."

"Okay, but what about the truck you stole?"

He stopped smiling then. "I did steal the truck, and I shouldn't have done that. I really didn't think I was stealing it at the time, though. I was planning on giving it back. Then I guess I just sort of slowly began thinking of it as mine and finally I forgot I'd stolen it. Until I saw you."

We were both quiet a minute.

"Why did you really come to live way out here? That wasn't your plan when you rented that truck. Couldn't have been. I get that some people want to live out in the woods, and I can even understand that some people don't care about indoor plumbing. But nobody wants to live in a truck for the rest of his life."

He stared at his boots again. A minute ticked by.

"No, I didn't want to live in a truck the rest of my life," he finally said. "But I did want to feel alive."

"What does that mean?"

"I'm dead. I have no social security number, no job history, no license, nothing. I couldn't get a job if I wanted to. I couldn't rent an apartment or buy a house or open a bank account. According to the law, I don't exist."

"I don't understand."

He took a deep breath.

"Back in 1983, I went on a fishing trip up in Canada with my wife. We hadn't been married long. First trip together after the honeymoon. We had a great time. Best time of my life—though I guess I didn't know it at the time. One night when she was sleeping in the camper I couldn't sleep, so I went out to take a walk. You know, just to see what was out there. There was a full moon, so I could see fine, but in the dark I guess I got disoriented and I was walking around all night trying to find our campsite again. It was real remote, so I never even came upon any other sites where I could get help.

"She woke up the next morning and must have thought something happened to me since all my clothes and wallet and gear were all still in the camper, so she drove the camper off to where she could find a phone. You know, no one had cell phones then."

I nodded. I'd always thought of those times in my life where no one owned a cell phone as some of the best times. But I guess I wasn't lost in the Canadian wilderness.

"I was convinced that I found our campsite once when she was gone. I saw tire tracks in the dirt and in the morning light the area looked pretty familiar, but there was no camper, so I kept going. I was getting worried. I tore off the very bottom of my shirt and wrapped it around a twig on a bush near the water where we had been fishing. I figured someone would see it and realize I was alive and well out there and waiting to be found. Then I took off again.

"I guess I shouldn't have done that. I should have stayed put. That's what they always said in school when I was young. But I thought that was just for dumb kids. So I kept looking. I pushed on and all the while I was walking further and further away.

"There was a search, but somehow they missed me and I missed them. Three days later I came on a little cabin in the woods. By then I was half mad with hunger and dehydration and all scraped up besides, but I was so grateful to find that cabin. I was terrified of staying another night outside in the cold and I was convinced a wolf pack was following me and getting closer every day. So I broke in—wasn't anybody living there since it was a summer cabin and this was November—and I managed, somehow, I don't quite know how, to survive the winter."

He paused there to take a long gulp of water from an old army canteen.

"Then what?"

"So while I was scraping by on canned food I found in the pantry and a couple deer I managed to shoot with a rifle that was left in the cabin, the United States government was declaring me dead. If you ask me, it seems like they jumped pretty quick to that conclusion, but I found out later it was because of insurance money. My wife couldn't collect it with me alive."

"So she had them declare you dead?"

"She didn't want to. I don't think she had a choice. But that's getting ahead of the story."

I sat back on my stump motioned for him to continue.

"When spring came I waited a bit for someone to come to that cabin to rescue me. But nobody came. And I was just about out of food. So I packed up a blanket and a tarp and the little food I had left and started walking south. Seemed logical since Michigan was to the south. Figured I would have to either hit a town where I could get help or else hit the border at some point."

He looked off into the woods at some unseen troubles.

"That was a terrible journey. I had run-ins with hungry bears waking up from their winter hibernation with nothing around to fill their bellies but me. I was hounded by wolves. I was starving and delirious and cold. But I did eventually find a house. This old couple took me in and tried to nurse me back to health. But I had no identification on me and at that point I was hardly making any sense. My hair was long and I had a beard and I had lost probably more than fifty pounds, so I looked nothing like the picture that had been on the news when I went missing, so that old couple didn't make the connection. Took weeks before I could even speak to them. I couldn't even remember what had happened to me."

"But wouldn't they call the police anyway if some crazed man stumbled out of the woods into their house?" I interrupted.

"You'd think so, but if I remember it they were pretty poor and the house was pretty remote. Either they couldn't afford a phone or maybe there weren't even any lines out there. Though the guy did have a car. Once I was coherent and not right at death's door, he offered to take me into town where they could alert the police, but I still couldn't remember who I was or why I was there. I was afraid to leave the safety of the house and go back into the woods, even in a car. He didn't want to leave his wife home alone with me—I suppose I don't blame him. But eventually they needed to go into town to buy groceries. They left me in the house. When they came back they had brought a police car with them."

"Not a mounty?" I quipped.

He let out a mirthless laugh.

"No, not a mounty. Cop wrote down some information about me and then drove off. Nothing came of it. I had walked so far from where I originally got lost, I don't think anyone connected me with the news story six months before. Searches for grown men who disappear hiking are a lot less sensational than the ones they have for killers or lost children. Seemed like everyone had forgotten me.

"That got to me, you know? I didn't understand why no one was looking for me, why no one seemed to care if I was dead or alive. I didn't even want to get back home at that point. I was too depressed. As the seasons changed and summer eventually became fall, I could tell that the old couple wanted me out of their house. They were generous, but their patience was wearing thin. So finally I let the old man drive me into that little town and I found a job and lived in a basement under a restaurant. I worked and lived there for a few years."

"You never remembered how you got out there?" I asked incredulously.

"No, I remembered by then. Someone came into the restaurant one day who made the connection because I'd gotten my hair cut, shaved off my beard, and gained back some of the weight I'd lost. And when he started describing the incident it all sounded familiar, though it was more like remembering seeing something on TV.

"I did remember my wife and I knew I had to go back and tell her I was okay. I started making phone calls to try to find her. Our old number was out of service, so I thought I would just have to go to our old apartment to find out where she had moved. I saved up some money, bummed a ride to the border crossing at Sault Ste. Marie, and tried to come back to Michigan. But I still didn't have identification. I couldn't prove who I was. So the border guard wouldn't let me in.

"Took me a day or so to make it happen, but eventually I paid a guy to smuggle me in—in a Haul-It truck. I hid in the trailer under a bunch of boxes and made it back into the US and he dropped me off in Lansing to look for my wife. But she'd moved. I asked around at our old apartment building. A few people recognized me and remembered the story of my disappearance. They were the ones who told me I was dead. And they told me she had moved to Lapeer. I tried to rent a car, but no one would rent to me with no license. So I went to the police to show I wasn't dead and I needed my identification back. They suggested I get it back from my wife! I told them I was trying to, but no one would believe who I was!"

I shook my head at his impossible situation.

"One of the patrol men felt sorry for me, so he offered to drive me to Lapeer himself once he was off duty. And that's how I got there and found my wife.

But more than three years had passed. She'd re-married. She had a kid. She bawled her eyes out when she saw me standing at her door. But I couldn't get her back and I knew I couldn't stick around with her living a new life.

"She gave me a little shoebox that had my expired license in it and news clippings from when I disappeared and my watch and a few other things. She gave me some money. She told me how they had found that little bit of my shirt on the bush and they had also found some blood from a cut I must have had. When they couldn't find me they figured I had either drowned and sunk in the cold waters of the lake or been injured and died in the woods. They dredged the lake but didn't find my body. She said she'd decided I must have been set upon by wolves. I left her house that evening feeling more alone than I ever had in my life.

"After that I tried to get the legal ruling on my death reversed, but the judge said I was a couple months too late. The law was that a death ruling could only be reversed within three years. I couldn't get a new social security number or license or any-thing. And so I couldn't convince anyone to give me a job or rent me an apartment. Lots of people said they wanted to help me but that their hands were tied. Had to have those numbers and documents. It was the law.

"So I started to think about Canada again. I'd been able to live and work there in that little town because people felt sorry for me and they never asked me for papers or IDs. I thought if I could get back into Canada I'd be all right. I went back to Haul-It with cash in hand. I put fake numbers on the form and made like I couldn't locate my license. I re-member your boss didn't want me to rent the truck, but you told him we could just check out the license numbers I wrote down later."

A light switched on in my brain just then. "I remember that. I felt kind of bad for you."

"So I got the truck and drove it up to the Soo to cross back into Canada. But I couldn't get in. No proper identification. I couldn't convince anyone to smuggle me in and someone alerted the police that I was trying, so I took off in the truck and drove across the UP, just wondering what the hell to do."

"Why not just walk into Canada from Wisconsin or Minnesota?" I asked. "I hear anybody can do it even now. Must have been even easier back then."

"Yeah. Hindsight's twenty-twenty. I didn't have my head about me very well at the time. I just kept driving and driving and driving. I stopped once in Marquette to buy some supplies since I thought I'd be on the road a while. Got everything you saw in the back of the truck there and a bunch of food besides. Then I got on the road again. I drove around aimlessly for days, in and out of Wisconsin and all around the UP. I ran out of money. Then I ran out of gas. And that's where the truck is right now."

"I don't get it," I said. "You were terrified of even leaving a house and now you've been living in the woods in a truck for twenty-five years?"

"Yeah, it's strange, isn't it? The first week I hardly left the truck. But what else could I do? Eventually I knew the ground around here so well I didn't feel like I was out in the wilderness anymore. I wasn't lost. I knew where I was and I knew who I was, even if I didn't really exist to anyone else. I ended up close enough to a small town to walk in occasionally and trade work for things I needed. So I've been able to buy food to supplement my hunting. And frankly I'm pretty proud to be so self-sufficient. If the world doesn't need me, I need them even less."

In the silence that followed the end of his story, I heard birds calling. I felt the cold breeze on my face. I smelled the stew on the fire. I imagined a life out here alone.

"That's some story," I said. "Do you think that stew is ready? It actually smells pretty good."

He smiled then. "It is good."

He dished it out and we both blew across our steaming spoons. I slurped up the stew, which really was quite tasty, and thought about my earlier assessment of his life in the woods.

"I'm sorry I called you lazy," I said. "You're anything but lazy."

He shook his head. "Don't worry about it."

We finished the stew in silence and drank up the instant coffee and then I looked at the clock on my phone.

"Shoot. I have to get going, man. I'm not even sure where I left the tow truck."

"I know where it is," he said. "It's barely out of sight of the Haul-It. You did a lot of wandering around in the wrong direction once you got out."

"You saw me the whole time?"

"Sure did."

"Why'd you let me wander around so long?"

"Why do you think?" he laughed. "I was hoping you wouldn't find the truck and you'd leave!"

I laughed then. "Well, could you point the way back to the tow? I have to get on the road. Long drive home."

"Sure thing."

We walked a very short distance over even ground and I did indeed see that I had wandered around for nothing. Once the leaves were totally off all the trees, there would be a clear view of the Haul-It truck from where I had parked the tow. I pulled myself up into the cab and stuck the key in the ignition.

"Listen," I said, "is there anything you need? Anything I can get for you from town? Food? Clothes?"

He shook his head. "Nah, I'm all stocked up for now."

I hesitated. "Do you need any money?"

He smiled and shook his head again. "I don't need your money, pal. I don't need anything."

I furrowed my brow. "That realtor is going to want you out of here still, you know."

"Don't worry about him. He's scared to death of me."

"What if he calls the police?"

"I'm not worried. I don't even exist, remember?" Seeing the look on my face he added. "Don't worry about me. I've been taking care of myself for a long time."

"Okay, buddy." I turned the key and the engine grumbled to life. I shut the door. The man gave a little wave. Then I rolled down the window. "Say, you mind if sometime I come visit you out here? Not sure when I'd have the time, but sometime."

Now his smile touched even those sad pale blue eyes. "Sure thing, pal. If you can find it again."

He laughed, waved, and turned around to walk back to his campfire. I pulled out onto the dirt road and did a three point turn. By the time I looked back, he was out of sight.

As I made the long drive home that night, I thought about how much I would tell my boss. Seemed to me the less he knew the better. I'd tell him the truck was a lost cause, as good as dead.

And then I thought maybe I'd ask for some time off. You know, just to see what's out there.

THE DOOR

Wesley Hutton took two steps back from the canvas and narrowed his eyes. The deep horizontal furrows that had long ago taken up residence on his brow pointed to the floor. Thin lips that had been hanging slightly open were drawn tight, as though someone had pulled at an invisible string.

He was used to painting the bustle of European nights, the colorful chaos of Eastern marketplaces, the wild beauty of tribal cultures in northern Africa. For his entire career he had traveled to far-off lands to capture life on canvas.

Now he was old. Rheumatic. Spent. The desire to create was as strong as it had ever been; Wesley was not. He sat confined to his house and looked each day for something to paint, but the well of inspiration within these walls had run dry. He thought of the beautiful young women who used to come to his Paris studio to pose. Such wondrous, fragile, tempestuous youth. And here he was painting cold objects on a bare table in a Midwestern ranch house.

Wesley laid the canvas aside, sat on his stool, and stared blankly at the wall for a long time. As he sat, the weak February light moved slowly through the room as day progressed until finally it rested upon the wall in such a way as to suggest a door where there was none.

And why not? Why not a door?

Wesley removed the still life from his easel, replaced it with a blank canvas, and poked one long bony finger into the basket of paints beside him. He fished for a moment, then found the viridian green and squeezed some from the tube onto a fresh palette. He repeated the motion, adding cadmium yellow, alizarin crimson, Prussian blue, plus a little black and a little white. He sampled and blended with a palette knife, then chose a large round brush and dipped the bristles into his first color.

In bold brushstrokes he sketched out the wall, layering different shades and colors, giving it a depth and texture it did not have in reality. He added shadows and dimension and painted in a strip of floor. He switched brushes, added paint to his palette, wiped away a mistake with a white cloth. He worked on the featureless wall with more passion and skill than he had employed with the still life. And beneath his practiced hand, the wall came alive.

Then it was time to paint the door.

With a new brush, Wesley swirled together a fiery blend of yellow and red. He breathed deeply, touched the tip of the brush to the waiting canvas, and slowly dragged it downward. He began again from the top corner and drew the brush across the upper edge, then down the long right edge and across the bottom.

A distracting splash of bright color at the corner of Wesley's eye caused him to look at the real wall across the room. There on the wall was a large rectangle. It was mostly yellow with some red and a bit of orange, precisely mirroring the one Wesley had just created on his canvas. Mouth hanging slack, he approached the shape, reached out, and touched one yellow line. The paint was wet and a dab of it came off on his finger. Wesley rubbed the smudge with this thumb, filling the lines of his fingerprints. Then he returned to the canvas, dipped his brush once more into the paint, and, without taking his eyes off the wall, began to fill in the rectangle.

As Wesley painted the canvas, the rectangle on the wall slowly filled with color until it was a solid yellow shape streaked with red and orange. When the last vestige of white canvas had disappeared, the old artist sat down heavily on the stool and stared at his rather unconventional creation. He began to wonder if perhaps he was unwell—high on paint fumes or perhaps even having a stroke. But beyond his heightened heart rate, he felt fine. More than fine. With precision and more artistic flourish than he had been able to summon in some time, Wesley laid in beveled panels to give the door some dimension, then added a doorknob in bronze and burnt umber. Then he left the room and waited for his painting to dry.

The next day, Wesley entered his studio. The door was very clearly three-dimensional now, the optical tricks of painting shadows and highlights somehow transformed into a reality. In wonderment, Wesley placed his hand on the knob and a thrilled shiver ran through his body when the metallic mass pushed back at his flesh. He wrapped his fingers tightly around it and turned it slowly. The knob spun then stopped, as all doorknobs do, but when Wesley pulled, the door did not open. He pushed instead, but it remained fixed in position.

Wesley slumped in an old tattered armchair. He stared at the door. The light changed slowly until evening, when it failed.

"Why is it so dark in here?" Wesley's daughter Meg stood in the studio doorway.

Wesley didn't seem to hear her.

Meg switched on a lamp. "What's this?"

"Hmm?"

"That door. Why did you paint a door?"

"I painted it."

"Yes, I can see that you did."

Wesley did not say anything.

"Listen, Dad, I have to get going but I just wanted to check in. I left some Chinese food in the kitchen for you. Want me to put it in the fridge?"

"Um...sure."

She gave him a long, hard look. "Why don't you try and get more sleep, okay? And not in that chair. I'll see you again in a few days."

He nodded absently. He heard the front door open and close and lock.

A lock.

Wesley rose from his chair and carefully added a keyhole and an ornate skeleton key to the painting. On the wall beyond the canvas, the objects gradually appeared just as the door had. Though his fingers ached to try the lock, he resisted. Instead, he ventured outside, tromping through deep snow to the west side of the house where he estimated the painted door must be. But there was nothing there. He went back inside, shrugged off his coat, and walked back to the studio, trailing snow behind him.

When the painting was finally dry and the key stuck out from the wall, Wesley reached with his trembling fingers and twisted it in the lock. It turned, clicked. He gently squeezed the cold metal knob and turned it with a flick of his wrist. The latch moved and the painted door creaked open, revealing an enticing sliver of golden light.

Wesley pressed the impossible door into the space on the other side of the wall and a bright room came into view. The walls were lined with shelves over-flowing with ancient books and manuscripts. Two great leather chairs and a low, imposing mahogany table stood like sentinels atop an elaborate woven rug and Wesley could hear the faint sound of a ticking clock. Warm yellow light poured in through long, narrow windows as though it were a summer after-noon rather than an evening in this unending winter.

He took one step into the room then remembered his boots. He fumbled with the laces a moment, then slipped out of the cumbersome things and placed them in his studio just beside the yellow painted door. Then he shuffled in on silent stocking feet and shut the door behind him.

Starting at the shelves immediately to his right, he glanced over the leatherbound tomes lined up like brownstones. Such a library. Had it always been on the other side of the wall, just wanting a door in order to be reached?

Overwhelmed, Wesley lowered himself onto the edge of one of the brown leather chairs. There on the mahogany table before him was an enormous book, its leather cover nearly the same color as the table upon which it rested. Wesley opened it and there, on the first page, was the first painting he had ever executed as a young man: a watercolor of a sailboat at a dock—he knew precisely which dock in a small fishing village where his family vacationed the summer of his seventeenth year—painted in the manner of a person who knows what he wants to do but does not know what is necessary in order to do it. His breath caught on something in his chest. He remembered how his mother had praised his work and how he had loathed it.

Slowly turning the pages, Wesley saw the next painting he had attempted, and the next, and the next, until it was quite apparent that they must all be there in the enormous book. Paintings he had burned in disgust, paintings he had given as gifts, paintings he had sold to keep the electricity on, paintings he had traded for a junky car or a new pair of shoes. With each page, Wesley saw his technique developing, his medium and his subject matter changing, his style evolving.

He had never taken the time to consider his body of work as a whole and what he saw astounded him. His life had always felt piecemeal. A move to this city. A marriage. A move to that city. A child. A commission here. A lean year there. A divorce. A stagnation. A breakthrough. Canvases of color to mark the passage of time, but nothing to trace a line of purpose through his life. No rhyme or reason. Just flitting like a butterfly from one thing to another.

Now as he saw his entire life's work on parade, he saw the faces of people he had not meant to paint. On the body of a street musician in Brazil was the likeness of his grandfather. The face of his mother graced the varied forms of French dancers, Nepalese washerwomen, and Slavic barmaids. His father appeared as a London businessman and as a stern Bedouin shepherd. His beautiful wife was everywhere during the early years, noticeably absent during the later years, and then reappeared as every sensuous woman he ever painted after the divorce. His lovely daughter Meg was every little girl in every far-flung town that had been more important to him than she was.

As he neared the end of the book, the likenesses disappeared. The figures that populated his paintings no longer had faces at all, just blank blobs of color to indicate a head. More impressionistic, more abstract, more removed from reality. Then he saw the still life he had completed just days before. Then the yellow door. Then nothing.

Wesley ran his wrinkled hand over the smooth picture, shut the book, and slid back in the leather chair wondering what came next. There were no blank pages at the end of the book. No room for more. Had he painted his last?

He was nervously running his hand along the arm of the chair, pondering his next move, when something brushed up against his leg. Looking down he saw a sleek black cat had entwined itself among his ankles. He bent over to pet the creature, but it dashed away, taking cover behind a heavy brocade curtain that fairly shimmered in varying hues of deep, rich red.

Taking in the curtain and the books and the quality of the light, Wesley determined that this was a room he could paint. He was not done yet. With a sense of relief, he turned back to the yellow door to retrieve his supplies from his studio, but before he reached it a pitiful mewling from behind the curtain redirected his attention and his progress.

He crept instead to the place where the cat had disappeared and lowered his arthritic body, wincing as his knees made contact with the hard floor. A small black paw poked out and batted at his hand. Wesley wiggled his fingers playfully to try to draw the cat out of hiding. The paw emerged again, batted at him once more, then disappeared into the luxuriant folds of fabric. Another wiggle of fingers, then the sharp pain of claws and teeth in flesh as the cat went in for the kill.

With a yell, Wesley reclaimed his hand from the cat's mouth and clutched it to his chest. No longer feeling so generous to the menacing black creature skulking in the curtains, Wesley gripped the drape firmly with his uninjured hand and swept it aside with as much noise and power as he could muster from his kneeling position. But instead of being greeted by the satisfying sight of a terrified and fleeing cat, he came face to face with a small red door, perhaps two and a half feet tall and almost that wide. It called with the same compelling force of the painted yellow door. Forgetting his plan to return to his studio for his canvas and paints, Wesley turned the knob and pushed it open.

Peering through the opening, he saw only a deep darkness at first, so great was the contrast between the bright library and whatever lay beyond this second door. Then ghosts of shapes slowly took form, like molecules gathering, contracting, becoming a solid mass. And then they were trees.

A thin wisp of a breeze reached for him from the other side and carried with it the faint scent of earth. Wesley leaned forward, hesitated for the space of a breath, then crawled through the doorway. The feel of the ground beneath his hands and knees, the smell of forest, the very act of crouching down in this bestial posture propelled Wesley's mind to the nearly forgotten days of his boyhood, the days before he had ever picked up a paintbrush, when scrambling around in the north woods was part of his everyday routine, a mode of travel to be enjoyed regularly after schoolwork was done and before the evening meal would be shared.

Then as he struggled to stand, Wesley felt all of his age. He winced as bones and joints assumed their normal positions once more, and looked back at the place from which he had emerged. Golden light from the library shone through the opening, though perhaps a bit dimly. Before him, soaring slender trees wore the first blush of budding spring leaves. Fog created a silken backdrop to the dark trunks leaning into each other, softening their shadows. The curved, graceful lines of young saplings drew Wesley's eyes to a faint V in the ground and all at once he heard the tantalizing sound of trickling water.

Taking a step, Wesley received a sharp reminder that he was not prepared for a walk in the woods. He picked a jagged stone from his damp sock and thought he had better go back through the library into his studio after all to retrieve his boots. But when he looked back to the door in the rocky hillside a part of him resisted. What if he went back for the boots and the magic of the painted door was spent? What if he could not get back into this incredible dream?

Wesley leaned up against a tree trunk and re-moved his socks. He tucked one under the small door in the hill to keep the wind from shutting it and hung the other over a nearby branch where it would be easy to see, a beacon to call him home. Then he made a careful descent down a soft path strewn with brown pine needles toward the small stream running through the earth. It tumbled over smooth rocks laced with moss and drew Wesley's eyes ever further from the place he had come. He wanted to follow it, wanted to see where it emptied, wanted to reach the end of things.

Surely there was an end. And what might be there?

So Wesley walked. Assisted by a series of willing rocks and stumps and trees, he picked his way along the stream. He walked for what seemed a very long time, though he did not tire. No sound of birds or wind could be heard—just the relentless rhythmic trickle of water on stone. Then Wesley finally e-merged beyond the forest into an open space. The rocky bottom of the stream gave way to sand, and as the fog thinned Wesley could see that he was headed toward a vast lake stretching out past the horizon.

Gentle waves licked with clock-like regularity at the wet sand shore, and where the stream emptied into the lake the waters quietly contended with each other for the right of way. The shoreline continued to the left and to the right as far as he could see. The sky was a blanket of low, gray clouds, one folded upon another, until it merged with the water in the distance.

Was this it, then? The end of the road? The end of his impromptu journey through the yellow door? Nothing but endless water?

Coming upon the lake felt like coming upon the final page in the book. What had it all been for? His life, his work, this pointless passage into some hidden realm. There seemed to be no reason for any of it. He had not garnered fame or much admiration as an artist. He had not improved the world. He had not even been a good husband or a good father. He had lived entirely for himself, following whims wherever they led him, making and breaking friendships as it suited him. And now he was an old man with nothing to paint and nowhere to go.

He must have missed it along the way. If he went back to the library, back to the enormous book of paintings, perhaps he could figure out where it was, where he could have turned down a different road or given a different answer or asked a better question. Perhaps it was hidden in the layers of paint laid upon the canvases that marked his days. If he found it, he could go back through the yellow door into his studio, into his life, and make it right, make it so the book did not end, so the stream of his life did not simply empty out into a vast and nameless water.

With new resolve, Wesley turned away from the lake and retraced his steps through the woods. The journey back along the stream was uphill and significantly more difficult for the old man, and he began to wonder just how long he had been gone. Trees that had offered him a helping hand before now snagged his shirt, pulled at his arms, slapped him across the face. Roots stretched out to trip him. Stones seemed determined to cut his bare feet, slow his steps. But finally he saw a dirty white sock gripping a crooked branch and the dim light from the library through the small door in the hillside.

Relieved, he dropped once more to his knees and crawled through the cave-like opening back into the book-lined room. He dragged his socks in with him, firmly shut the little red door, and drew the brocade curtain to cover it up once more. He pushed himself up from the floor and settled back into the leather chair. He quickly flipped past the first painting to the second, another watercolor, this one of farmland not far from his boyhood home. The next ten or twenty were much the same—the work of a young man trying to discover what he cared about and how to interact with those subjects with paint and paper. He studied them closely, looking past the issues of technique that had occupied his mind on the first pass through the enormous book, and instead searching for clues about his mental and spiritual state when he had painted them, for what he had missed even as he was so keenly observing his world.

Soon he reached the paintings he had done in art school—experimental pieces he had been very proud of then, but that he could now see were full of the worst kind of pretension. As the pages slowly turned, he recalled the way he had parroted his instructors to gain their favor. He remembered the way he had perfected the art of criticism thinly veiled in a fake compliment and directed toward any student by whom he felt threatened.

With the turning of the next pages, Wesley found himself in his twenties. Beautiful women in varying states of undress replaced the natural subjects of his earlier work. These were the years he had explored the strange new landscape of the feminine heart, years he had fallen in love with nearly every pretty face that looked his way. Years when, even as his world seemed to open up with a move to New York City, his inner life had contracted violently, until he was consumed almost entirely by personal pleasures.

Meeting Caryn had changed that to some extent. His world expanded to include two people then, and they quickly made plans to float through Europe on her father's dime and what little money they could make through Wesley's art and her writing. The paintings in the enormous book showed a sudden shift. The decaying remnants of ancient civilizations collided with the vitality of modern culture in the great cities of Europe. Piazzas in Rome, castles in Switzerland, monasteries in Spain, all populated with interesting people at whom Wesley had looked so closely, though without ever really seeing any of them. He painted houses he didn't live in, people he didn't know, churches he never deigned to enter. He painted the shells of things, but not the things themselves.

Soon he came upon his first years of fatherhood, that golden time of unexpected love and unexpected hardship. Growing close to the new girl in his life on the one hand, drifting further from her mother on the other, until Caryn felt like a stranger and Meg like a chess piece in an unfriendly game. The hues of his paints darkened. His subjects never smiled. But there was always that small hopeful childish element to give a bit of light—young faces not yet broken down by life. Always Meg's face.

Wesley had left Meg in her fourth summer, no longer able to pretend a love for Caryn he had not felt in years. And though late in life he had reconnected with his daughter and made amends, he had missed the most important years of the girl's life. He hiked across Asia, Egypt, and Morocco. He lived with tribal people with whom he could hardly communicate, sometimes went weeks without speaking to anyone. And he painted it all. He painted the life he was not brave enough to live.

Page after page, his life slipped by until he came once more to the still life of stones, piled as though to mark a grave. And then the yellow door he had walked through only to be met with the stark reality of his wasted life. He closed the book, slid back in the chair, and listened to the steady ticking of the clock. One minute ticked by, then another, and then the black cat leapt silently onto the mahogany table and sat impertinently upon the book, looking at Wesley through narrowed eyes. They stared at each other a moment, then Wesley heard the sound of a car door slam in his driveway.

Meg. It must be morning. Wesley rose from the leather chair and walked around the table toward the yellow door. He was about to put his hand on the knob when the cat meowed at him. He turned to see the creature rubbing up against the red brocade curtain, each pass moving it a little so that Wesley could see the corner of the little red door. But he would not be distracted this time.

Wesley turned the knob and pulled, but the door did not open. He heard his front door being un-locked.

The lock. The key. He'd left it in the lock on the studio side.

Footsteps in the hall.

He knocked on the yellow door. "Meg? Meg? I'm in here."

Footsteps in his studio.

Meg's muted voice. "Dad?"

Footsteps past the yellow door.

He knocked again and yelled. "Meg! I'm in here. I left the key out there. Can you unlock the door?"

Muffled sounds. Shuffling.

"Dad?"

He pounded with all his strength. "The key, Meg! It's in the yellow door!"

Wesley put his ear to the door. He heard the soft sounds of crying, then a silence, then a long, deep breath.

"Meg?"

Footsteps out the studio door, down the hall, then Meg's shaky voice on the phone drifting further and further away.

Then he knew. He could not go back.

The cat meowed again from across the room. It had moved the curtain aside completely and now sat imperiously by the little red door. A tear slid down Wesley's cheek and he covered his mouth with one bony hand to hold back the despair that threatened to break free. He looked around the library once more, no longer gold. A pale and failing, sickly yellow. And he knew it was time to go.

With a last lingering glance at the enormous book, Wesley lowered himself to the floor and opened the little red door. The breeze drifted in, cooler than he'd remembered it, and he crawled through. Then the wind picked up and slammed the door behind him.

CLEAN

Lindsey Travis leaned against the cold metal line of washing machines and stared at the swirling colors in front of her until it made her already unsettled stomach roil. She looked away from the dryer and slowly drew in a breath through her nose, held it a moment, then let it tumble past her lips. She should have eaten something, but nothing was appetizing anymore. The mere smell of her grandmother's fridge when she'd opened it that morning nearly made her vomit. She had gladly escaped the stuffy house to do the wash at the Laundromat just a few blocks away.

Now she eyed a yellow plastic chair along the wall of windows that faced the parking lot. Slipping her purse from atop a washing machine, Lindsey made her way to the chair, one in a long line of similar chairs in red and orange, all faded from a few decades of direct sunlight. She sat down heavily and fished her phone out of her pocket to check the time.

She held the phone loosely in her lap with one hand. The other she slung over her head as she leaned back to rest it on the glass behind her. Exhausted. That's all she ever felt anymore.

It had hit her all at once a few weeks ago. Her grandmother had had to wake her up several times for school as she slept through her alarm. She'd fallen asleep in her afternoon classes more than once. Caffeine had no effect except to make her feel sick to her stomach. She had just figured she had mono or something.

Eventually her grandmother had insisted on bringing her to the doctor. It was what that doctor had told her that ruined everything.

The phone vibrated in her hand and she checked the number before answering.

"Hey, Trish...The Laundromat...Yeah, definitely. I checked again this morning...No...I can't... Because they need a parent to sign something...It's a permission thing, I dunno...No, you have to be eighteen...I thought of that, but I don't know where I'd get one...Trust me, I've already looked into all this...Yeah, I know...I should be done here in another hour...I don't want lunch...No, I don't even want to go in there with you. The smell would make me puke...Okay, sure. See you tonight."

She clicked off the call and stared into space, hardly believing she was having conversations like this.

The dryer buzzed and Lindsey pulled herself to her feet. She kicked her white plastic laundry basket into position below the machine, opened the round door, and raked the hot clothes out with her hands. Satisfied she hadn't missed anything small, she shut the door and propped the basket on the line of washing machines. She reached in and pulled out a fistful of underwear.

One by one, panties of all colors and patterns were held up, shaken out, then folded, crotch up, left side, right side, until several short stacks of these neat little packets lined the side of the basket.

Lindsey held up a pale yellow pair with tiny orange and purple flowers. It was edged in flirty lace and a prim purple bow marked the center front of the waistband. She stared at them a moment, then folded them. Up, left, right. She placed them on the top of a stack and continued with the rest. T-shirts were next, then socks and a couple pairs of shorts. She tucked the stacks of clean clothes back into the basket and opened a washing machine. She fished towels and jeans from the drum and shoved them into a dryer. She put four coins in the silver slots, pushed them into the machine, and selected high heat.

When the dryer was tumbling again, Lindsey went back to the basket of clean clothes. After staring at it a moment, she carefully slid the yellow panties with the orange and purple flowers from its stack and threw them in a nearby trash can. She could never wear those things again.

She looked again at her clothes and felt tears well up in her eyes. How long before none of them fit her anymore?

The bell above the door jangled and Lindsey swiped the tears away and turned to look at the newcomer. The woman pulled a collapsible cart behind her and walked with a red-tipped white cane toward the machines. Lindsey watched her deftly maneuver the narrow aisle between the washers and dryers. She came to a stop not far away and Lindsey suddenly realized she was not a woman at all.

The legs visible between the black heels and the knee-length skirt were most certainly a man's. Lindsey could see this even through the dark nylons. And the torso and shoulders and chest, they also belonged to a man. And if there were any doubt left in her mind those doubts were gone once Lindsey took a good look at the woman's face. Though crowned with a feminine bob and flanked by dangling earrings, the shadow of stubble across a muscular jaw was most certainly a man's.

"Excuse me," the woman said to her in the voice of a man. "Is this machine taken?" A manicured fingernail tapped metallically on the hood of the washer.

"N-no," Lindsey managed in a hoarse whisper.

"Great." And with a gleaming smile, the newcomer opened it up and began transferring things from the cart into its cavernous mouth.

Lindsey watched closely and saw that everything, down to undergarments, was women's clothing. She pulled out her phone to text her friend Trish.

There's a blind drag queen here. Seriously.

Trish's response came quickly.

No there isn't. No way.

Lindsey typed furiously.

Swear.

She waited for a response.

Pic or I don't believe you.

Lindsey switched her phone over to camera mode and tilted it up surreptitiously, trying to get the newcomer in the frame. Then she realized it didn't matter how obvious she was if her subject couldn't see anyway. She held the phone out in front of her to get the drag queen and the cane in the frame, but hesitated before clicking the shutter.

She turned her phone off and dropped her hands to her sides, imagining what the coming months had in store for her. She knew her schoolmates would be taking pictures of her, or if not pictures, surely they would be dropping their eyes and their voices and whispering about her. This person, no matter how comical to her, didn't really deserve a picture passed around or posted on the Internet. He was just someone who dressed weird. Really weird.

Instead of gawking more, Lindsey turned off her phone and sat back down on her yellow plastic chair. It wasn't long before she started to zone out. She stared across the room, conscious of the tumble of colors at the periphery but careful not to fixate on the swirling clothes. All the same her stomach clenched and released as waves of nausea continued to wash over her.

"You're awfully quiet," a voice said through the fog.

Lindsey looked over to find the drag queen sitting two chairs down, angled toward her slightly.

"Yeah. I'm—I'm just thinking, that's all," she replied.

"What about?"

Lindsey examined the sunglasses. Was this person really blind?

"Nothing, really," she said. "Just stuff."

Her neighbor nodded.

"I think about stuff sometimes. Seems like that's all there is to think about sometimes. Stuff."

"What stuff do you think about?" Lindsey asked. What were the secret thoughts of a drag queen, anyway?

"Sometimes I think about work. Sometimes I think about my family. Think about them a lot."

"What's your family like?" she asked.

"I'm not really sure how to describe them. I guess you'd say they were pretty quiet folks."

"That must be nice," Lindsey said. She thought of the last couple months living with her grandmother, TV and radio blaring. The last few years she lived with her mother. All the shouting, the slamming doors. The time before the divorce. Arguments and the sounds of breaking—furniture, glass, bones.

"Not so nice," her companion broke in, "when you can't see. You like a little more noise then. I always wished one of my parents had played an instrument or been a little better conversationalist, you know?"

Lindsey nodded then realized her error. "I guess so," she said aloud. What she wanted to ask—What did your parents think of the fact that you're a transvestite?—she kept to herself.

"You play an instrument?" the drag queen asked.

"No. You?"

"No. Should've learned to play the trumpet, I always thought."

"You could learn now," Lindsey suggested.

"Maybe."

They were quiet for a few minutes, listening to the whir and tumble of the machines.

"Forgive me, sweetheart, but your voice sounds kind of young to be spending your Saturday doing laundry. Why aren't you sleeping in or out with your friends?"

"Needs to be done. Grandma told me I could stay at her place if I didn't create more work for her. So I do the laundry."

"I see. Just you and your grandma?"

"Yeah."

"Listen, I'm sort of a nosey person, so you'll have to forgive me, but why don't you live with your parents? Something happen to them?"

"They're divorced," Lindsey said.

"You don't want to live with one of them?"

"Dad moved away. Mom kicked me out."

"Oh, I see. You two don't get along, then?"

Lindsey expelled a puff of air. "Yeah, you could say that."

"I see."

After a few more minutes of silence, a washing machine buzzed.

"That's me," the drag queen said. "Don't suppose you might give me a hand here…uh…"

"Lindsey."

"Hi Lindsey, I'm Ruby."

"Rudy?"

"Ruby," she said, emphasizing the B.

Ruby lifted a hand. Lindsey shook it tentatively and said, "I can help you."

Ruby opened the washing machine and Lindsey opened a dryer directly across from it. When Ruby began to reach for the clothes, Lindsey piped up.

"I got it."

"Thank you. Maybe I'll make it home with everything this time around. Sometimes I drop a little something on the floor between the washer and dryer and I never notice it until the next time I want to wear it, you know?"

Lindsey nodded again. "Yeah."

"Then it's too late. I used to call the owner to see if anything ended up in the lost and found, but it seems in general people just steal stuff that gets left behind."

"That sucks."

"You said it."

Lindsey carefully transferred Ruby's clothes to the dryer, making sure not to drop any on the floor. She recoiled a bit at touching this stranger's underwear, but made sure everything made it safely across the three foot space between the washer and the dryer. She took the coins from Ruby's large hand, popped them in the four slots in the silver tray, and slid them in with a *clang*.

"What temperature?" she asked.

"Low, please," Ruby replied. "I don't want any of those knits to shrink."

Lindsey turned the dial and pushed start.

"Do you have anything else that needs to go in the washer?" she asked.

"Not today. Just one load at a time for me. Makes it easier to get around. I take the bus, so I don't want to be dragging all of my dirty laundry with me and taking up too much room."

"Why don't you have a washer and dryer at your house? Seems like that would be a lot easier with your…" Lindsey trailed off. Despite her parents' constant insults and finger-pointing, at school she had always been taught that pointing out flaws in others was rude.

"Limitations?" Ruby supplied. "Yeah, it would be easier. But I move around a lot. Just so happens this place doesn't have a washer and dryer. Next place might. But I'm sure not going to spend the money on them."

"Why do you move around so much?" Lindsey asked.

"That's a bit of a story," Ruby said. "How about we go sit down?"

They settled back down in the plastic chairs by the wall of windows. This time Ruby left only one seat between them.

"It probably has not escaped your notice that I'm not a typical woman, Lindsey," Ruby began. "I've been dressing this way since high school. Not in public at first. Just occasionally. But when I turned twenty-five I just thought screw it—I can't see the strange looks people give me anyway, so who cares? Sometimes I'll get a comment from some jerk, but most people are the type that are just trying to get through their day and if I don't bother them they don't bother me. But I don't dress this way for work. Just in my free time. Doesn't fly at work. Not around here. Maybe in a bigger city."

"So why don't you move to New York or San Francisco or something where you wouldn't stand out so much and you could dress how you want?" Lindsey broke in.

"Never held much appeal to me, I'm afraid. I'm a small town girl at heart. This is about as big a city as I can handle."

A machine buzzed.

"Oh, hold on a sec. That's my other load," Lindsey said as she rose from her chair. She opened the dryer and began to fold the jeans and towels. "So why do you move around so much?"

"Well, like I said, I dress like a man at work. But once an employer discovers my 'other life' if you will, they don't always like to keep me around."

"But isn't that illegal, to fire someone because of something like that?"

"Technically, but that's not the reason anyone ever gives. And anyway, it's not always me being fired. Sometimes it just gets too uncomfortable and so I leave. Find a new job, a new town. Move on. It's not so bad. I like meeting new people."

Lindsey considered this. "I wouldn't mind moving to a new town."

"Yeah? What's wrong with this one?"

Lindsey folded the last pair of pants and popped it on top of her stack. She removed the shirts and underwear from her basket and tucked the heavier towels and jeans in first. Then she topped them with the more delicate things and sat back down.

"I hate it here," she said simply.

Ruby waited for her to continue.

"My life sucks. My parents hate me, I live with my grandma, the guy I was seeing dropped me, and now—"

Lindsey choked back the emotion fighting its way out of her throat. Ruby waited quietly.

"Now I'm pregnant and I don't know what to do. I can't do this. My grandma will be furious when she finds out and I just keep thinking what if she kicks me out? Where would I go? And my friends are all going to be going to homecoming next fall and I'm going to be huge and I can't afford to buy all new clothes and I won't be able to finish school and—"

"Shh," Ruby slid over and put a hairy arm around Lindsey's heaving shoulders. "You'll make it, sweetie."

Lindsey shook her head. "No, my life is over now."

"No, it's not." Ruby gave her a squeeze. "How old are you?"

"Sixteen."

"There, you see? You're sixteen. Your life is just beginning. Things are bad now, but that doesn't mean they'll always be bad. You think it's easy being me? No ma'am. You think it's easy being anyone in this messed up world? Think again. Everyone has bad times. Everyone feels like giving up at some point. But life over at sixteen? Nonsense!"

Lindsey looked at her reflection on Ruby's sunglasses. The curved lenses made her creased brow abnormally large, her chin strangely small, her hair flat and lifeless.

"Listen, Lindsey, you'll get through this. You just gotta work hard, okay? And don't mind what people say. We all mess up. And in ten years, none of this will matter. When you're sixteen, ten years sounds like a lot, I know. But it'll go by in a flash, especially with a little baby."

The word *baby* set off a fresh wave of tears.

"I can't," Lindsey sobbed.

"Yes, you can, Lindsey." Ruby smiled and dug a pack of tissues from a purse. "People do it all the time. That's how all of us got here in the first place."

Lindsey couldn't keep herself from smiling a little when she saw the optimism on Ruby's face. She took the proffered tissue, mopped the tears from her cheeks, and blew her nose.

"I guess so," she said. She took a deep, slow breath. "Sorry. I didn't mean to freak out like that. I've been crying a lot lately."

"From what I understand, that's pretty normal," Ruby said. "You seen a doctor?"

"Once."

"I also understand you're supposed to see the doctor a lot. You got one of those books on what to expect?"

"No."

"Better get one. And get back to the doctor. And tell that grandma of yours."

"Yeah."

They sat in silence until Ruby's dryer buzzed.

"Need any more help?" Lindsey offered, though her own laundry was done.

"Sure."

They walked over to the dryer and Lindsey piled armfuls of dry clothes atop the line of washing machines.

"How do you fold your shirts?" she asked.

"Any old way you want to fold them, so long as they fit back in that basket of mine."

Lindsey held up each item, gently shook the wrinkles out, and folded each one precisely. She folded t-shirts, some stretchy yoga-type pants, a few light sweaters, but pushed the underwear into a pile for Ruby to fold. The two of them stood at the washers a few minutes, folding and flipping without a word. Ruby's clothes were quite a bit bigger than her own. And Lindsey began to think again about all the clothes she would have to start buying soon that she couldn't afford.

"I can put them in your little cart," Lindsey said when they were done. She leaned down and carefully stacked the folded items so they wouldn't wrinkle. When she stood straight again, Ruby held out a hand.

"Thank you for your help today, Lindsey. And the conversation."

Lindsey shook the proffered hand.

"I wonder if you would mind running over to the bulletin board near the door and telling me when the next bus will be here," Ruby said.

"No problem."

Lindsey trotted over to the front door, looked at the clock on the clerk's desk, and scanned the extensive bus schedule for a few minutes, trying to make sense of the tangled colored lines indicating various routes that crisscrossed the city. She finally located the right line and checked the table of arrival times.

"Should be here any minute, I think," she said as she made her way back to Ruby.

"I see," Ruby said. "It was sure nice meeting you."

"You too," Lindsey said.

She watched as Ruby methodically pushed the cart out the door. No sooner had she stepped up to the corner bus stop than the bus arrived. In a flash of metal and glass, Ruby was gone.

Lindsey leaned her elbows on the washing machines and buried her face in her hands. A few deep breaths later she straightened, slung her purse over her shoulder, and slid her basket of clean clothes off the washer and onto her hip. She pushed through the dirty glass door of the Laundromat and started the short walk back to her grandmother's house.

The clouds that had speckled the sky that morning had moved on and the sun beat down on her so that she was glad to reenter the dark house, even if there was no air conditioning. She could hear the television blaring some game show and knew without peeking into the living room that her grandmother would be in her recliner, covered in cats and holding a large bowl of cheese popcorn. Trudging up the stairs with the laundry basket, Lindsey tried unsuccessfully to imagine a baby in the midst of that scene.

She put the basket of clean clothes on her unmade bed and began transferring items into her dresser. Underwear and socks were tucked snugly into place in the top drawer, t-shirts in the next one down, jeans in the bottom.

Lindsey picked up the towels, intending to take them across the hall to the bathroom, but a flash of red made her stop. There at the bottom of the basket was a large red v-neck shirt and beneath that a pair of stretchy black yoga pants. Lindsey remembered folding both of them, stacking them with Ruby's things, and putting them in Ruby's cart. And yet, there they were, at the bottom of her basket.

Then she remembered the errand Ruby had sent her on to the bulletin board.

Lindsey sat down on her bed, held the gift loosely in her hands, and cried. They were not the tears of despair she had been crying since her visit to the doctor. They were not tears of joy. They were simply tears.

Eventually the tears were spent and Lindsey tucked Ruby's clothes into a drawer. She walked down the stairs into the living room and right up to the television, which she turned off.

"Hey!" her grandmother said as startled cats scattered to the corners of the room.

Lindsey took a deep breath. "Grandma," she said, "I have to talk to you about something."

10 DEGREES COOLER IN THE SHADE

I never really met Chet Currie. Not formally. You rarely get into a real handshake and eye contact situation in this line of work. Mostly you might notice someone new, a face you didn't see in the last town, and eventually you just know that person's name or you don't. Don't know how it happens exactly. Some hang on for a year or two and become like part of the equipment—like you'd notice if they weren't there because things just wouldn't work right. Others drop off after a month and you forget they existed at all— that is, if you knew who they were to begin with.

So I couldn't tell you exactly when I became aware of Chet Currie. But I do remember the first time we spoke. I had grabbed a pop and a Polish sausage from Ronnie's stand and sat down at a picnic table under the overhang by the east toilets to eat and watch the people flow by. Always found that to be the best part of the day. Getting out of the hot sun, resting my voice a moment, and watching the whole country shuffle along past my spot.

Boys chasing each other. Girls glancing a-round to see if there was somebody cooler they could be talking to. Moms dragging dog-tired kids by their arms. Teenagers with hands in each other's pockets. Fat guys getting fatter on fried Snickers and elephant ears. Redheads with lobster-red arms from too much sun. Every type of person there is in this world, I got to see them all, in every size town in practically every state.

I think that day with the Polish sausage and the pop and Chet Currie was somewhere up in Michigan during the front end of a weeklong county fair. It was supposed to be a hot week, but that didn't seem to keep the crowds away. Farmers came with their prize pigs and horses and steer. Little girls clutched rabbits and chickens and sucked on frozen lemonade. Little boys led goats into stalls and then took off for the ticket booths. And then, of course, there were all the people from the surrounding towns coming in for the tractor pull and the demolition derby and the carnival rides.

I ran a ring toss game. You know, where you try to get a ring over a bottle to win a piece of junk you'd never give a second glance in a store. Once people had stuffed themselves with enough cotton candy and popcorn and candy apples so that they hardly knew where they were anymore, they'd shell out crazy amounts of cash for a chance at a ratty pink teddy bear or some dumb hat. And I took their money knowing full well that the easier the game looked the harder it really was. At the end of the week I had my share from the director's take and it kept me in food and cigarettes and gasoline for the RV.

I knew I was never getting rich on this gig, but it was a decent enough way to earn a living. Besides, I wanted to see the country and it seemed a pretty cheap way to do it. I had no roots, no electric bill, no nylons or high heels. I felt free. All those people who rode the Ferris wheel and the tilt-a-whirl, they were at the fair for a day, maybe two, then they went back to the office or the classroom or the worksite. I got to go to the fair every day. In my world it, was always summer.

I don't think Chet Currie had the same idea about the whole thing. While I sat in the shade with a little smile on my face, he sat with a little scowl on his. It's not a rule or anything, but I don't generally start up conversations with men—too many of them take that as more interest than it really is—but for some reason I thought maybe Chet Currie had something on his mind he needed to get off. I took stock of him: skinny, tan, glasses, balding but with some longer hair that was plastered to his head with sweat. He didn't seem like a threat. He seemed like a guy who probably didn't have a lot of friends.

"So, I see you've moved to the spinning strawberry this week. You like that better than the dart throw?"

He didn't look at me or make any sign that he'd heard me at first, so I took another bite of sausage. I was mid-swallow when he piped up.

"Lateral move," he harrumphed.

"Yeah, why's that?" I asked.

He swirled the melting ice in his large Styrofoam cup.

"Just a different kind of pain in the ass," he said.

I sipped my drink in silence and considered how to end the conversation on an up note and get the hell out of there.

"At least you get to see those smiling kids."

He snorted.

"Most of the time they're just whining and complaining. Or the little ones are crying. Stupid parents just staring at their phones. Pay no attention to 'em so I have to deal with 'em."

"Not most of them, though, right?" I said in a hopeful tone.

He finally faced me. "They're all little jerks in the making."

I popped the last bit of bun into my mouth and stood up.

"Well," I said around my half-chewed food, "at least you don't have to keep blowing all those balloons up."

He scoffed.

"See you around," I said as I turned to go.

"Hey, wait," he said after me. "Your name Cindi?"

"Yeah."

"I'm Chet Currie."

"I heard."

"Oh, yeah? From who?"

"I dunno. Just heard."

I worked out my shift as usual and didn't give Chet's comments too much thought most of the night. From my position in the fairway I couldn't see many kiddie rides too clearly. Once in a while I'd see the little train for just a second. But mostly I kept my eyes on the people milling around my game. You could never be too careful. There's always bad people around, waiting for any chance they can get to take something that ain't theirs. People change in the dark. Those same people I watched for fun when I was taking a break I had to watch like a guard dog once the sun went down. But hey, it's all part of the job.

I saw Chet again when I was closing down my stand. One or two stragglers were dragging themselves out the gate and all the rest of the carnival staff were turning off the power and clicking the locks. A few guys from a nearby prison gathered trash in front of push brooms. Everything was resetting for the next day and Chet was loping toward me with a big smile on his lean face.

"Where you going in such a good mood?" I asked.

"Bar. Where you think?"

I nodded.

"You wanna come?" he asked.

I shook my head. "I'm headed to bed."

"Suit yourself."

Now that we knew each other, this sort of exchange went on between us every night of that week. Each time I declined the invitation he looked a bit bummed. And then that bummed look turned to an annoyed look. Don't know why he needed me to go to the bar with him. Plenty of people went to the local bars every night. He would have all the company he could want.

The week ramped up and we all did our jobs more or less until it was Friday, one of the busiest nights of the fair. By that time we were all a little tired, a little frazzled, and those people with tempers were all out of patience. I was always very careful about what I said to certain folks once the weekend came. Especially on a hot week like that one.

By Friday night I was ready to collapse into bed when I got back to my RV, but I took the time to wash off the sweat of another day in the sun. I combed through my clean, damp hair and braided it, then brushed my teeth and set the coffee pot for the morning. Tomorrow would be the biggest, busiest, loudest day of the fair and I for one was looking forward to Sunday when I could sleep in before the dismantling started and we dragged it all to a new town. When I finally got under the covers it was after one o'clock and I'm pretty sure I fell asleep within moments of closing my eyes.

I woke some time later to pitch dark night and no indication of what had woken me. There was no rain on the roof, no thunder and lightning, no dog barking, no voices. No sound at all. I closed my eyes again and then I heard it. A light knocking on the window above my bed.

I stayed where I was at first, my sluggish brain not willing to process what a knock on my window might mean. I was drifting off to sleep again when the knock came louder. I pushed up onto my elbow and parted the mini blinds with my fingers. Nothing. I pressed my forehead on the glass and searched the dark beyond it. Nothing. Then the knocking moved to my door.

Now fully awake, I rose, put on my robe, and walked a few paces to the locked door of the RV.

"Who's there?" I asked in a voice scratchy from too much shouting and not enough time to rest it.

Silence answered me. Then another knock.

"Hello?" I said louder. "Who is it?"

I heard a voice answer me, but it was muffled by the door and by something else. I cracked the door and immediately knew what that something else was.

"Chet? What are you doing here?"

Chet Currie stood before me in the porch light looking like he'd lost a fight. His jeans and his tank top were filthy, his cheek was bruised, and his lip was bloodied. But it wasn't just a fat lip that made his voice sound strange through the door. He was obviously very drunk.

"Hey, Cindi," he slurred. "I thought this was my place."

"Then why were you knocking on my window and my door?"

"I wasn't. I was just trying to see…"

He trailed off and looked around helplessly.

"Where's your trailer?" I asked.

Chet looked both ways down the line of RVs and then shrugged. "I thought it was here."

I stepped out to the ground in my bare feet and tied my robe tight against the chilly night air.

"You're going to have to do better than that," I said. "I'm not knocking on every door in this place. You got a key?"

He fumbled for his pockets and I noticed that his knuckles were scraped up and the fingers of one hand looked nearly twice their normal size.

"Listen, why don't you come in here a sec and let's get you cleaned up a bit, then we'll look for your trailer."

He looked as close to grateful as he could with that face and followed me into the RV. I flicked on the light and motioned to him to sit down. I clicked on the coffee pot I'd prepared earlier, then I wet down a washcloth in the sink. After carefully wiping the raw skin on his knuckles, I rinsed the blood and grime down the drain. I dabbed around the angry bruise forming on his cheek and by the time I cleaned up his lip the coffee was sputtering to a stop. I poured him a cup and set it on the little table next to him.

"So, you want to tell me what happened?" I said at last.

"I dunno," he said, shaking his head. "I just…this guy…" Then he tried again. "There was a fight is all."

"Well, anyone could see that. What happened? You get jumped or something? Should we call the police?"

"No, no," he said quickly. "Don't need the police. Just a fight is all."

"Are you sure? Have you seen yourself?"

His face darkened. "No police."

"Okay, okay," I said, holding up my hands. "You start it, then?"

He didn't answer, but the look on his face said plenty.

"Well, what happened?" I asked again.

"Never mind that," he said. "They won't bother me again. Took care of that."

I didn't like the sound of that, and I really didn't like being in the same little room with Chet Currie drunk and angry.

"Well, let's go see if we can find your trailer."

"I don't need no help," he said. He tried to stand but stumbled and careened into the countertop.

"I think you do, Chet. Just tell me what your trailer looks like and we'll find it."

He put his head in his heads. His voice wavered a bit as he said, "It's white."

"They're all white, Chet. What other colors are on it? When make is it? What's the license plate number? Which row is it in?"

He started to cry into his palms. "I dunno."

"All right…well, would you know it if you saw it?"

His head gave a feeble nod under his hands.

"Okay. Finish that coffee and we'll just start at the beginning of the park and walk until we find it, okay?"

He put the mug up to his lips and grimaced, then moved it to the uncut side and took a small sip. We sat in silence as he slowly drank down the entire mug. I snuck a look at the clock and when I saw that it was after four in the morning I suddenly felt very tired. I had to get Chet Currie out of my hair or tomorrow was going to be a very long day.

"You look real pretty tonight," he suddenly said in a serious voice.

I took the empty cup from his trembling hand, rinsed it, and set it in the sink. Then I held my hand out to help him up.

"Let's go."

I held onto his arm to steady him, but it was obvious from the get-go that he needed more support than that, so I draped one long arm over my shoulder and held onto his forearm with one hand and his skinny waist with the other. It was a shaky start, but once we had our feet on the ground outside and got a bit of a rhythm going, we made pretty good progress. Soon we were at a corner of the large grassy lot where all the carnival personnel lived out the week.

Step by tortured step, we passed through the lines of RVs and pop-ups. I stopped in front of each one, let Chet get a good look at it, and then moved on when he shook his head. A time or two I was sure he was going to say, "Yes, this is it," but then he'd notice something—a lawn chair or a dream catcher in the window—and shake his head again.

I started getting a little panicky when I could see the end of the very last row, but finally, after what had to be an hour of looking, he got a little smile on his face and nodded.

"That's it," he said.

"You sure?" I asked.

"Yeah, that's the one."

He pulled his arm from my shoulder and it felt like a hundred pounds had just been lifted off my back. He tried the door but it was locked.

"You got your key?" I asked.

"Course I do," he said defensively. He checked his left pocket and came up empty. He tried to check his right pocket but winced when he tried to put his swollen fingers into it. He patted it with his left hand instead and then tried to get that hand in it. When that failed he looked at me helplessly. I was beyond ready to go back to bed to try to get a few hours of sleep before I had to open up my game again, so I stuck my hand into his pocket, felt the key, and pulled it out. I gave it to Chet, who I was pretty sure was trying to leer at me suggestively. But in his drunken and disheveled state it looked more like he had just entered the pig barn.

"Go on," I prodded him. "Open the door so I can get back to bed."

The leer turned to sneer and he made a few clumsy attempts to fit the key into the hole. Impatient, I grabbed it out of his hand and shoved it into the lock myself. But it didn't turn. This was not his trailer.

I let out a curse. Chet looked apologetic. He looked over the last few RVs in the row and then said, "I guess we missed it."

"*We* didn't miss anything," I said. "I'm going back to bed."

My compassion all worn out, I started back to my own trailer.

"Wait," he said with an edge of desperation. "Can I use your bathroom?"

"You're a guy. Just go over by those trees over there."

"I think I'm gonna be sick."

"Well, I don't want you sick in my trailer. Look, Chet, I did my best and now I need to get some sleep. I'm afraid you're on your own now."

I walked quickly back to my trailer now that I wasn't weighed down by a drunk. I went in, made sure the door was locked, turned off the light, and shuffled back to bed. I laid there for what felt like ten or twenty minutes, wide awake, wondering where Chet would end up sleeping it off. I felt a little bad, but I had done what I could. I wasn't about to let him back in my trailer to puke in my toilet or sleep on the couch.

I peeked through the blinds again and saw the barest hints of the coming day—a grayness that was starting to creep into the black sky. Sunrise was probably still an hour off, but there was no way I was going to be getting back to sleep that night. I was debating whether or not to just get up and warm up the coffee I had brewed for Chet earlier, when pounding on my door startled me to my feet.

I rushed over to the door in my nightclothes, opened it a crack, and hissed through the opening.

"Shhhhhh! What is your problem?"

The door swung out of my grip as Chet Currie wrenched it open. He grabbed my wrist and yanked me from the trailer. My foot caught on the way down and my ankle twisted when I landed hard on the ground. Then his long, battered face was suddenly an inch from mine.

"You wanna know what happened tonight?" he said in a low growl past the dried blood on his lip.

I shook my head quickly.

"Sure you do. You kept asking."

"It's none of my business."

"If I tell you what happened tonight, are you going to let me crash at your place?"

I shook my head again. "No, Chet. You can't stay here. I don't care what happened."

He glared at me.

"Let's go."

He pulled at me and I pulled back.

"Let go."

He pulled harder.

"I just want to show you what happened, that's all. Since you're so curious."

In hindsight, this is where I should have screamed and woken up everyone in the RVs around us. I can't say exactly why I didn't. I'm not a screamer. Maybe it's because whenever my father got this drunk it was always best to just let him rage until he slept it off. Any arguing got you smacked. And really, Chet didn't seem all that dangerous. I had a good thirty or forty pounds on him. I was used to fending for myself. And not an hour ago he couldn't stand on his own two legs. Maybe he'd gotten a second wind, but it couldn't last. So I let him pull me away from the trailer park toward the fence that surrounded the carnival grounds.

The gray light was getting a little stronger now, but it was still hard to see beyond the circles of yellow made by the floods. Chet obviously knew where he was going now. He couldn't find his trailer, but wherever he was taking me was fresh enough in his mind. We walked quickly to the back fence behind the fun house. A section of the fencing had been torn away, bent at an awkward angle, and it was here that Chet stopped.

He pulled at the fence and pushed me through the small opening. I had to crawl on my hands and knees in the dirt. A sharp part of the chain link snagged at my shorts and cut into the skin of my thigh. I was just getting to my feet on the other side when Chet Currie slithered through the opening and gripped my wrist again. He pulled me up to a loose panel on the back of the fun house, pushed me down onto my knees, and then pressed my head against the dirt.

"There, you see him?" he asked.

I couldn't see anything.

"You see him?" he asked again, louder this time.

"No." It was barely a whisper.

He dropped to his knees beside me and pulled up the loose panel allowing me to see what should have been empty space beneath the fun house floor. But it wasn't empty. A face stared back at me from the shadows. I couldn't tell who it was, but it was definitely a person.

"You seen that guy before, Cindi?"

"I...I don't know."

"Sure you do. That's your buddy Ronnie."

I couldn't speak.

"You wanna know what happened, right? Ronnie was shooting off his mouth tonight at the bar, saying I touch those kids on my ride. I don't touch nobody. I hate those kids. I hate that ride. I hate this damn carnival. And I hate Ronnie. Don't need nobody spreading rumors about me. I don't touch those kids. So now nobody'll spread rumors about me. Shoulda kept his mouth shut."

Down there on my knees with my face in the dirt looking into those dead eyes I tried to imagine what might happen next. The sun was coming up. Soon people would be up. Someone would come by soon and drag Chet to the director's office and call the cops. I just had to bide my time.

"I punched him right there in the bar and we had it out for a bit. Thought he'd won, so he left. But you know how I did it?" Chet said.

He pulled a large knife from his back pocket and flicked open the blade. It glinted slightly in the growing light and I felt my heart beat a little faster.

"I followed him out, followed him back here. Then I came up behind him like this."

Chet got behind me and pulled me upright. He snaked one skinny arm around my waist and held the knife in his swollen right hand.

"I put my knife right up to his throat like this."

I felt the blade at my throat.

"And I slit his lying throat," Chet hissed in my ear. "So he won't be spreading rumors about me anymore."

I tried to keep my breathing under control.

"I never spread any rumors about you, Chet," I said calmly. "I know you don't touch kids."

I couldn't see his face, but I felt his muscles loosen a little bit. He still held me in his grip, the knife at my throat, but he was deflating a little behind me.

"I really like you, Cindi." His voice once more sounded scared and sad and helpless like it had when couldn't think of what his trailer looked like.

"How about I let you sleep on my couch and I'll let the boss know you're not feeling good and they can find someone else for your ride today? That sound good?"

He heaved a sigh behind me.

"Thank you, Cindi."

He hugged me tightly with the one arm around my waist and the knife still at my throat. And then I felt a sharpness and a wetness dripping down the front of my nightshirt and I couldn't scream. Chet stood up and I slumped over.

"Here, Cindi," he said and he pulled at my arm.

But I couldn't get up. I stayed on my knees in the dirt, my face to the ground, a puddle of blood forming below me. Chet yanked at my arm.

"Cindi?"

Then he rolled me over. His face was a kaleidoscope of emotions. Confusion and anger and sorrow and fear all mixed together in a horrible mask. He pulled at me some more, whispered my name, looked around frantically, then realized what must be done. He lifted the loose panel on the fun house and shoved and pushed me into the dark space below next to Ronnie. He pushed the bloodied dirt underneath with me, scuffed at the ground with his boots, and then dropped the panel and stumbled away. Then there was silence.

The sun did finally rise and a sliver of light pierced the dark space where I lay. But it couldn't reach me. I lay there in the dark, part of the equipment, and waited for someone to notice I was gone.

THE ASTONISHING MOMENT

"We kept saying this is the shadow; and we thought now it is over—this is the shadow; when suddenly the light went out....How can I express the darkness?"
                    ~Virginia Woolf

The sun had not yet chased the last of the stars away when Sawyer Reynolds got into his kayak, pushed out from the beach near the mouth of the river, and glided smoothly onto the glittering surface of Misery Bay. He had spent the last night under a sky choked with stars, camping illegally on the beach, but nobody seemed to care to give him any trouble. Now a week beyond Labor Day, it was no longer peak travel season along the Lake Superior shoreline.

This was precisely why Sawyer had chosen this time of year for his trip. That and the fall colors that were already beginning to kiss the tops of the maple trees this far north. But the lack of people was the main thing. After months of serving vacationers at a hotel on Mackinac Island, he was more than ready to get away from people in general and needy tourists in particular. Here he would not have to dodge wobbly children veering around the street on tandem bicycles. Here he would not have to give anyone restaurant or fudge shop recommendations. Here he would not have to work twelve hours a day to keep up with all of his duties. It was just him, his lens, and what felt like the very edge of the known world.

True, there was Canada—a vast country way up there across the cold, blue inland sea, with cities and streets and houses and people. But there was still a wildness to this place that could not be denied, a tempting isolation that called him to abandon his life, get lost, start again in some remote woodland glen where no white foot had ever been placed. Oh, to have been born half a millennium ago when it was all still out there, waiting to be seen for the first time by Western eyes, as if the act of seeing was what made it all real.

Now with the dawn about to break and no one in sight, it was easy for Sawyer to imagine that he was alone in the wilderness, embarking on a voyage that might fundamentally change the world. If his kayak were but a sleek birch bark canoe he'd crafted with his own hands and his camera a leatherbound journal scribbled upon with a quill pen, he could almost convince himself.

The lake was nearly still, and as the kayak cut smoothly through the glassy surface of the water tiny ripples began traveling out into the distance. The waning moonlight reflected in the water shivered. Sawyer gently paddled, alternating left, right, left, right, and the shiver became a tremble. When he was about fifty yards or so from shore he began to paddle harder. If he wanted to make Copper Harbor by the end of the day—a long haul even in calm conditions—he would have to push himself. He'd given himself just one week to reach Grand Marais, where he would meet a friend he'd bribed into picking him up and spending half the day driving him all the way back to his car, which was parked in a lot about twelve miles northwest of Ironwood. And so Sawyer huffed and pulled and matched the beat of the paddle with his heartbeat.

On this side of the Keweenaw peninsula, the sun would rise over trees that attempted to hold back the daylight a little longer, but Sawyer knew that the gray cast of dawn was enough light to get started. An early start meant fewer waves, less effort.

He glided along in an intense, though not uncomfortable rhythm, past the north end of the bay and into deeper water. For one hour, then two, he carried on as the eastern sky brightened. Then all at once, the sun crested the trees and Sawyer could feel its warm glow on his right side. He checked his watch. Every day the sun rose later and set earlier, and today the big orange ball clocked in well after 7 AM, even accounting for the trees. Sawyer smiled in satisfaction, estimating that he'd already managed about ten miles—halfway to his first stop for the day.

Even in an aerodynamic sea kayak, though, Sawyer couldn't keep up that kind of speed indefinitely. Now he rested his paddle across his lap, stretched out his shoulders, and took a breather. Shading his eyes against the sunrise, he could see the rugged cliff-face to the east covered in a thick blanket of trees. He couldn't believe his good fortune that for a third morning in a row it appeared that he would have ideal weather for this trip. Sure, the nights were a little chilly, but the cool, calm, sunny days were perfect for paddling.

After a few minutes' rest, Sawyer put on his sunglasses, gripped his paddle, and pushed ahead. Over the course of the next couple hours of paddling, the sandstone turned to beach and then to a mere ribbon of sand beyond the forest and then back to cliffs. An occasional inviting cove or dark cave caught his eye, but he locked them away in his memory. He didn't have time to lollygag on this trip. This one was all about speed. Next year he'd go sightseeing.

Sawyer's stomach clenched with hunger when he finally saw a good place to make landfall and eat breakfast. An unexpected green lawn appeared out of the trees and widened as the kayak approach the mouth of the canal. Two great arms of stone reached into the water at manmade angles and at the end of one stood a light.

Sawyer turned and ran his kayak aground on the beach south of the jetty. He released the spray skirt from the watercraft and slid out. It took him just a moment to get used to having land under his feet again, then he dragged the kayak a little further up on the sand and opened the front compartment where he kept his rations. He pulled out his water bottle, a granola bar, and some string cheese. Try as he might to make his small breakfast last, the food was gone in just a couple minutes and his water bottle was running low. He walked back to the lake and filtered some water, then the sound of the water filling the bottle reminded him that he needed to relieve himself.

The next several hours followed a similar pattern. Paddling hard, resting briefly, a few sips of water, and paddling again. The shoreline undulated gently along to his right as the sun climbed in the sky until it was as high as it would go. With little to see beyond trees and water and an occasional house, Sawyer let his mind wander widely through currents of memory to the first time he saw Lake Superior as a boy of eight.

His small family was "doing the UP" as his father put it. They had planned stops at the Soo Locks, Tahquamenon Falls, the Shipwreck Museum at Whitefish Point, and a boat cruise along Pictured Rocks National Lakeshore. Sawyer could still remember the moment the car came around a bend and the glittering blue lake first stole his imagination. Ever since that time he had looked for ways to get that far north again. He'd dabbled in hiking, but viewing Superior from the land just wasn't enough. So he bought a kayak.

At first he got a bit of flack for the purchase. Most kids wanted a car, and certainly a car would have been more useful to him in his post-industrial southern Michigan town. Still, there were small inland lakes nearby and streams that were big enough for him to traverse in his shallow boat. And as the years went by, Sawyer upgraded his watercraft and checked many bodies of water off his list, including four of the five Great Lakes. He'd kayaked Superior before—though just for one glorious day. His current trip was the most ambitious one he'd yet attempted.

Suddenly Sawyer came to and realized that he had no idea what time it was or where he was in relation to his itinerary. He looked at his watch. Both hands pointed staunchly at the twelve, but a look at the sun, which by this time was hovering behind a thin haze, caused him to second guess his timepiece. As everyone does, he rattled the watch on his wrist and put it to his ear. He heard nothing.

Still, there was nothing to be alarmed about. Sawyer reached back and cracked open the lid to one of the storage compartments in his kayak. He fished blindly for a moment until his hand hit his cell phone. He carefully pulled it out and turned it on. The display read 4:23. But it couldn't be 4:23. He'd never even stopped for lunch, never—until this very moment when it hit him hard—even felt hungry. Could he really have paddled for more than seven hours unawares?

Thoroughly confused, Sawyer tucked his phone into a zippered jacket pocket and looked around. He was much further out in the lake than he'd intended. The water swelled and rolled beneath the hull in rhythmic waves. Far off in the distance to the east—or was that south?—he saw the strip of land he had been following. There really was no telling just where he was now. He might have passed Copper Harbor by entirely without even noticing it. Though surely he would have seen other boats—freighters at least, if not a sailboat or two. He certainly couldn't be the only one on the lake. The shipping channels were always busy until the weather turned bad in November.

There was only one thing to do. Sawyer turned his kayak toward the strip of green floating on the horizon and began paddling straight toward it. Once on land he would be able to get his bearings.

The closer Sawyer got, the more apparent it was that the landmass he was aiming at was not actually attached to the landmass he'd thought he'd been following. He quickly pulled a folded map from his inside jacket pocket and examined it. The only island near the Keweenaw Peninsula was Manitou Island, a magnet for migratory birds but of little interest to anyone else.

If this really was Manitou Island, Sawyer could stop there to eat and then turn back to get to Copper Harbor (which he was now sure he'd missed) in order to stay the night and bulk up his food supply. One night in a motel would do him good after so much exertion. And he had been looking forward to a shower. The temperature and humidity had risen throughout the day and Sawyer was sweating under his windbreaker.

Caught up as he was in his reverie about times gone by, he had not only taken his eyes off the land, he'd taken them off the sky. Only now that he had altered his course did he see the bank of gray clouds that had been piling up behind him in the northwest. A distant rumble whispered and Sawyer took a moment to allow the reality of his situation to come to the front of his mind.

A storm was coming. He was perhaps two miles from an uninhabited island. And if his mind had wandered for even ten minutes more that afternoon he might have missed the island entirely and found himself caught in open water holding a metal bar in a thunderstorm. His stomach did a little flip at the close call, then his tired arms began to pump harder, to drag him closer, foot by foot, to the land that would save him.

But the nearer he got to the shallow waters around the island, the choppier the lake became. The storm front bearing down on the lake was already churning up the cold waters, dredging the sandstone lakebed, stirring up the deep places that wanted to remain silent and hidden. The water beneath him was no longer the crystalline blue glass of morning. It was gray and brown and white, and it was splashing him, soaking his hair, reaching behind his sunglasses into his eyes, slipping beneath his collar, and running down his back. In one chilly moment the lake had changed from beguiling to behemoth and that strip of green seemed to get farther away instead of closer. Sawyer found it harder and harder to maintain his course as the current worked to sweep him eastward.

He could not miss this island. No matter what happened, he could not miss it.

With every minute that ticked by, the clouds edged closer and the thunder grew louder. The very air around Sawyer seemed charged with electricity. And then, without warning, the sun was blotted out. All was gray and even Sawyer's yellow kayak lost its color. The rising sense of desperation he had been feeling since he'd spied that gray wall advancing over the water reached the tipping point and became outright panic. He pulled against the tide, but he knew without a doubt that it was winning, it was driving him into a lake that had claimed perhaps thousands of lives over the centuries.

Then, when he thought it could not possibly get any grimmer, the light seemed to go out from the world entirely. He could still feel the waves rocking him, could still feel the pull of the paddle against the heartless water, could still hear the wind. But he could see nothing. Then the rain began.

A moment later he was blinded as a streak of lightning rent the sky above him and a spine shattering crack of thunder roared at him from the clouds. Then the blackness returned. Sawyer felt his heart reverberating and his insides deflated under the weight of compressed terror.

He would not reach the island. No matter how hard he tried, he would miss it.

Then somewhere out of the blackness he heard a small voice.

"Boozhoo!"

"What?" he shouted at the voice.

"Boozhoo! Aandi ezhaayan?"

He was imagining it.

"Bangan, niijii. Bekaa."

Lightning lit up the sky once more and for a moment Sawyer saw the form of a woman in a canoe. Then she was gone, replaced by another boom of thunder.

He was hallucinating.

But then there was a firm hand upon his.

"Noogishkaa. Aandi ezhaayan?"

"I can't understand you!" Sawyer shouted into the storm. "What are you saying?"

"Niin Anaamisagadaweshiinh nindizhinikaaz. Aaniin ezhinikaazoyan?"

"I don't know what you're saying! We have to get to the island!"

More lightning flashed around them and Sawyer could plainly see that the woman was a native American, though she looked nothing like the native people he remembered seeing on the reservation on that long ago trip to the Upper Peninsula with his family. They had been dressed more or less just like he was, in jeans and t-shirts and with trendy hairstyles. This woman wore a beaded buckskin dress and cape and her long black hair was braided. With another flash of light from the heavens, Sawyer saw that the boat she was kneeling in was made of birch bark.

He thought perhaps he was no longer sitting in his kayak being tossed about on the angry waves, but instead must be sinking to the bottom of the lake, drowning and delirious.

"Niiskaadad. Ashibishidosh."

Another flash of lightning and Sawyer saw the woman's arm was raised, her finger pointing in the direction he was trying so hard to travel.

"Minis Manitou."

"Manitou! Yes, Manitou Island! That's where I'm trying to go. If we miss it we're screwed!"

In the blackness, Sawyer felt the woman's hands upon his arm, then his paddle was wrenched from his fingers. The bottom dropped out from his stomach, but then the woman's arms were around him, pulling him. Without quite knowing why, he released the spray skirt from the kayak and scrambled into the birch bark canoe. A wooden oar was thrust into his hands.

"Wewiib."

Sawyer cut into the lake with the oar on the left side of the boat and the woman behind him did the same on the right. Now with the power of two people, there was finally some progress toward the direction that Sawyer now could only take on faith was the correct one, as he could no longer see any land. But for the occasional lightning, he could see nothing at all.

The two paddled fiercely until Sawyer was on the very edge of surrender to the storm. Then something scraped the bottom of the boat and he allowed himself a moment of elated hope.

"Aki!" the woman shouted.

They both leapt out of the canoe and hustled through the waves to the shore. They dragged the boat up the beach and into the woods, which seemed to close in around them. Then the woman was tipping the canoe over. She grabbed Sawyer's sleeve and pulled him beneath the boat. And there they crouched as the storm raged and whipped up the trees overhead.

A black lightheadedness overtook Sawyer's exhausted body and he collapsed in a heap upon the ground underneath the low roof of the canoe. The next thing he saw was a shaft of golden light in the space between the side of the upturned canoe and the ground beneath him.

He listened intently. He could hear a bird nearby. Beyond that was the sound of gentle waves lapping at the shore. And beyond that was nothing. No storm. No wind or thunder or rain. Just the palpable quietness of wilderness.

Sawyer tipped the canoe on its side and shielded his eyes against the rays of sun hanging low in what he was fairly sure was the eastern sky, judging by the quality of the light. Morning.

He straightened his legs, stretched out the kink in his neck, rubbed his aching shoulders, and then glanced over his surroundings. He was hemmed in on all sides by conifers. Enormous white pines towered overhead and below them stood friendly looking fir trees and stiff spruce with a bluish cast. Light filtered through the boughs like sun through stained glass windows and suddenly Sawyer thought to thank God that he was alive.

Then he remembered the woman.

"Hello?" he shouted

The only response he got was a fluttering of frantic wings as a small, startled bird took off overhead. Thinking that she must have gone to the shore to get water, Sawyer began to pick his way toward the sound of the lake. Beneath his feet a carpet of dead pine needles muffled his steps and in just a moment he was at a steep slope of rock and roots leading down to a sandy beach. Try as he might, he did not remember scrambling up this slope in the storm. But then, who could remember much beyond the dark dread?

He navigated the drop to the beach and walked straight to the water's edge. The lake that had tried to kill him the day before looked pleasant and enticing once more and Sawyer wished for his kayak. It was probably in Canada by now.

He scanned the shoreline in each direction, but there was no sign of the woman.

"Hello?" he shouted again, but his voice dissipated into the blue sky.

He walked down the beach a ways in each direction, then back to where he had left the canoe. Or where he thought he had left the canoe. But the little clearing in the trees was empty. He was sure that was the right slope, the same one he'd come down. But then he was not so sure. For a few seconds he felt his heart start to beat a little faster at the thought of being stranded. Then he remembered the lighthouse.

He was on an island that had had a lighthouse since the 1800s. All he had to do was follow the shoreline until he reached it. Then he could contact someone who might help him. He only wished he had his kayak, or at least that birch bark canoe, which would have gotten him to the lighthouse so much faster than walking on sand would. And he wished he knew what had become of the woman.

He checked the position of the sun again as he patted his pockets. His cell phone could confirm the time of day so that he was sure he was headed in the right direction at least. And if he was improbably lucky, he might even be able to alert the authorities of his predicament to speed his rescue.

When the patting failed to reveal the device, Sawyer stuck his hands into his pockets. But they weren't his pockets. This wasn't his windbreaker at all. It was a vest which fit snugly over a loose white linen shirt he did not own. Sawyer looked down at his attire, utterly confused. Instead of jeans he wore trousers of lightweight wool that were tucked into tall leather boots.

He closed his eyes, opened them, then closed them again and shook his head vigorously. The lack of food and water must be causing hallucinations. He had to find that lighthouse fast.

Though he knew that he would probably regret it in a week or so when he was doubled over in pain in the bathroom, Sawyer kneeled at the edge of the lake and drank deeply of the cool, fresh water. It was so clean that many who regularly sailed its waters drank straight from Superior with no ill consequences. Sawyer's stomach was not accustomed to it, so he carried a water filter in his kayak, which was now long gone. Still, it would be better to be sick later than collapse from dehydration now.

When he had slaked his thirst, Sawyer gathered many large stones from the beach and arranged them in a circle away from the water's edge so that he would know the spot if he returned to it. He thought about forming the words "help" and "lighthouse," but it seemed so clichéd and cinematic. No one did that in real life. Besides, he was not utterly desperate yet. He could survive in the woods for a few days if he needed to, he was sure. Wild blueberries, raspberries, and blackberries could tide him over.

When he was satisfied with his place marker, Sawyer began his journey. With the sun before him, he took step after labored step through shifting sand, across terraced slabs of sandstone, and over rounded rocks worn smooth from centuries of refinement by wind and water. The lighthouse was on the eastern-most point of the island at the end of a long, narrow peninsula. Sawyer reasoned that since he had nearly missed the island entirely, he must be very close to the light station. But after he had walked for what seemed like an hour or more, he had seen nothing beyond trees. At each bend he expected to come upon it, but was met with only more beach or more stones.

By the time the sun had risen to its zenith, the thought occurred to Sawyer that perhaps he was not on Manitou Island at all. Perhaps he was wrong. Nothing, in fact, was sure at the moment. But what else could he do but keep walking the shoreline? He had to come upon some human activity eventually.

The hours stretched on and Sawyer's feet ached and burned within the tall leather boots. He'd nearly forgotten the mystery of his clothing as he hiked but remembered it when he went to remove his shoes to dip his sore feet into the cold lake. Could a hallucination last this long?

And then he saw it. Not the lighthouse. But the circle of stones he had made on the beach that morning. Lightheaded and disbelieving, Sawyer stumbled up to the shape and sank to the ground inside the circle. He felt tears forming in the corners of his eyes and wiped at his face with his sleeves. No, not his sleeves. What were these clothes? Who was that Indian woman? Where was the lighthouse? Where was the canoe? Where was his cell phone? Where was he?

Sawyer covered his face with his palms and then pressed the heels of his hands into his eyes. He had to pull himself together. He had not survived that storm only to perish in the North Woods. He was taking a few deep, slow breaths when he heard a familiar voice.

"Inini wabiska, ambe."

He looked up and saw the woman in beaded buckskin beckoning him from between two trees at the top of the slope. Relief washed over him like a river and he got to his feet, though rather unsteadily. In a few steps he stood beneath her.

"Don't you speak English?" he asked. Perhaps there might be some very elderly Ojibwe people in Michigan who still spoke only their native language, but not someone as young as this woman. They all spoke English.

"Ambe," she said again, and turned toward the forest.

Sawyer followed.

As they walked a narrow trail through the woods that was at times nearly invisible, the woman did not look back at him. Sawyer struggled to keep up. In addition to stumbling over roots on the ground he tripped over his thoughts. Why was he dressed so strangely? Had this woman changed his clothes when he passed out from exhaustion the night before? Had she stolen his phone and his watch? Where was the lighthouse?

"This *is* Manitou Island, right?" he finally said to the woman's back.

She turned toward him and pointed at the ground. "Minis Manitou."

Sawyer nodded.

"Isn't there a lighthouse on this island?"

She glanced back at him and smiled, but kept walking.

Eventually they came to a clearing in the woods where a small circle of wigwams stood. Perhaps two dozen people were milling about, engaged in various tasks.

Sawyer stopped in his tracks. No Ojibwe lived on Manitou Island. No one lived here. And anyway, no one lived in wigwams anymore.

He patted down his attire again, thinking of his expensive camera at the bottom of Lake Superior and wishing at least for his cell phone in order to take a picture.

Then his hand lit upon something he had not expected. From a pocket inside the vest, Sawyer pulled a leatherbound journal he had never seen before. He untied the laces that held it shut and flipped through the rough-edged pages, which were covered with words and drawings. He looked closer at the text and saw that the penmanship matched his own. He began to read the words, which he had never read, and they were instantly familiar to him, as though he had just put them down the day before.

Have made contact with a group of native women at a temporary shelter as they dry wild rice and berries for winter. They call themselves Anishinaabe. One woman in particular has been very welcoming to me and has offered shelter, though I think her companions may feel suspicious toward me. Am attempting to learn as many words as possible, but this language is a difficult one. I do know that the woman who has befriended me is named for a bird, perhaps a wren, but her name is so long I cannot even attempt to reproduce it here.

The woman he was reading about stood in the door of a wigwam and said in a clear voice, "Beindigain."

And in that moment, Sawyer forgot his kayak, forgot his cell phone and his windbreaker, forgot the lighthouse. He forgot the things he could not see. Because they were not there. They were not real. They never had been.

MEMORY MAN

Detroit is a city with a long memory. Though most folks I know want to forget. Only they can't. Can't forget the past. Can't forget the glory days. Can't forget the rot and decay. I thought maybe we'd be better off if the whole world could forget what Detroit once was. Then maybe we wouldn't feel so bad about what it is.

But that wasn't what I had to forget exactly. And that did seem a tall order for just one man, even if he was miraculous.

It's a strange story, I'll give you that. I wouldn't believe me if I was in your shoes either. All I know is what I saw. So that's all I'm telling you.

My brother, Mike, first told me about the Memory Man one night when I was nine. We were at the window of my upstairs bedroom looking out at the long rows of glowing streetlights and all the bright houses where parents were still up doing whatever it was parents did once they confined us kids to our

- 187 -

rooms. At the time, I knew I would never need his services. What did I have to forget?

"Why do they call him the Memory Man if he can't remember nothing?"

"Because he takes your memory and forgets it."

"Then why isn't he called the Forgetting Man?"

"I don't know. He's the Memory Man. That's all. He's the guy you pay to take your bad memory and forget it for you."

"How much does he charge?"

"I don't know. Whatever it costs."

I thought it all sounded like a bunch of lies. How could someone else forget a memory for me? Didn't make no sense.

Anyway, it was easy as anything to forget. I forgot stuff all the time. Forgot my homework at school, forgot to feed the dog, forgot to flush the toilet, forgot to brush my teeth. I didn't need any help forgetting nothing.

I didn't know then that when I turned thirteen I'd have more to forget than I could even remember. Like the night my dad left and the night I missed those free throws. The times I had to skip dinner and the sight of my mother's boyfriend slapping her. The day my rotten dog ran away. The day Shannon broke up with me. The day I found out she had been seen making out with my best friend.

I started writing things down—just in case. I figured someday I could just hand the Memory Man the list and that would be it. But first I'd have to find him. If he was real.

Problem was, I never knew anyone who had actually seen the guy. And I didn't know anyone who knew anyone who had seen him. It was always a cousin's sister's boyfriend's ex-stepmom. Just a few too many links and a few too many known liars in the chain. Felt a bit like maybe I had a better chance of meeting someone who knew where Jimmy Hoffa was than someone who had actually seen the Memory Man in the flesh.

Then one day I was wasting time in a parking lot not far from my house when I saw a lady looking all around like she didn't know what direction to go.

"Hey, lady. You lost?"

She spun around to look at me.

"Yes, I think I am."

"Where you going?"

"I don't remember. That's the problem."

I had heard of Old Timer's disease, where people got so they couldn't remember anything. But this lady wasn't so old.

"What's the matter with you?"

"I just saw the Memory Man and I guess I must have told him too much. I don't remember where I was going when I ran into him."

"Yeah, right. The Memory Man? He ain't real."

"Oh, you so sure about that?"

"Okay, then what'd you tell him?"

She looked at me like I was being dumb on purpose.

"I don't remember, kid. That's the point."

My palms started to sweat.

"Where is he?"

She looked around and screwed her face up.

"Well, I saw him back behind the party store around the corner, but I don't know if he's still—"

I took off running so fast I could barely hear that lady as she yelled after me, "Be careful what you tell him!"

I reached the party store in thirty seconds flat and ran around the back, twisting my ankle in a huge pothole. I sucked in some air between my clenched teeth and rubbed my leg as I looked all over the alleyway. I limped behind the overflowing dumpster and kicked at the bags of trash piled around it. I checked the other side of the rotting fence. I hobbled around the whole place then checked inside. No one there except a clerk whose eyes followed me around as I looked down each aisle.

"You seen a lady and a guy talking around here a few minutes ago?" I asked him.

He blinked once. "You gonna buy something, kid?"

I went back out the door and scanned the street. But no one was around.

I couldn't believe I had missed him. So I decided that lady must have been crazy. The Memory Man was just a lie and she was just some harebrained lady who didn't know where she was.

But time is a funny thing, and by the time I was sixteen, I was a believer again. And I was glad I hadn't found the Memory Man that day at the party store, because now I had a whole bunch of new stuff that I wanted to forget even more. Shannon had been replaced with Michele. Free throws had been boxed out by that fight I lost to Antonio with half the school watching. Mom getting slapped was almost better than Mom on meth.

I'd lie in bed at night, looking out that same window, trying to get a fix on the few stars bright enough to beat the light pollution, and I'd pray that the Memory Man was real, that I'd find him if I just kept my eyes open and asked the right questions.

Whenever anyone brought him up I quizzed them on the details. Was he black or white or something else? How old was he? Did he have a beard? How long was it? What was he wearing? What part of town was he in? Was he thin or fat? Did he talk? How did you know it was him?

I got lots of answers. But this answer didn't match that one and this other one made both of those impossible. For every detail I thought I'd nailed down, three new questions came up.

By the time I was in high school, I had filled a whole notebook with lists and interviews and memories. Tucked inside was a city map covered with little stars and dates scrawled in black ink where people thought they'd heard he was. Sometimes I'd pull the map out when my brother Mike was out of the house, which was more and more, and I'd look for patterns in the markings, like a detective trying to catch a serial killer. But I was no closer to finding him.

I didn't realize then that you didn't find the Memory Man. He found you.

Once I was out of school, I didn't think quite so much about him. People who couldn't forget the past were weak, tied to things they couldn't change. I was moving on and I didn't need to spend my time looking for an old man to help me do it. I was too busy looking for something else—a job.

I applied all over the city at just about every place I could think of that wasn't a factory or a fast food joint. I was sure I was a pretty hot commodity and made for greatness. Smart, handsome, and ready for anything the world could throw at me. I'd avoided getting in with the wrong crowd, just like my teachers had warned me. I never hung out with Mike's friends or got caught up with my mom's supplier. I kept my nose out of other people's business and earned good grades. I did everything they told me to in order to better myself.

I had dreams.

People with dreams worked in offices and wore suits. People with dreams could afford new Cadillacs and good cigars and big houses in the suburbs. People with dreams moved out of Detroit.

But dreams are dangerous. Everyone tells you to have them, so you just can't help yourself. Teachers tell you that you can achieve anything if you just put your mind to it. And then they say the same thing to the guy sitting next to you, who you know is really just one deal gone bad away from prison. So you figure they have to say that, like it's part of their job description. Only in your case, they really mean it and when they talk to the loser next to you they've got their fingers crossed in their pockets so it really doesn't count. It's part of your job to create that dream and feed it and chase it.

And that dream grows inside you like a cancer.

You start to think that you'll be the one who makes it, the one your teachers will point out to their students years later as the guy who proved it was possible. That's the worst kind of dream. The kind that can change everything if it only came true. The kind that has the power to destroy you when it doesn't.

That's the dream I had as I typed up my résumé and wrote my letters and read job listings. I knew I wouldn't be on the top floor right away. I wasn't that delusional. But I'd gotten my degree and scored well and I knew I was a fast learner. I was ready to get moving. The world was waiting for me.

Only I didn't get any calls. Not one. It was as though when I sent those résumés and letters out I hadn't addressed them at all, just climbed one of the towers on the Ambassador Bridge and let them fly into the wind. I was waiting for the ringing of a phone and all I got was the empty sound of indifferent silence.

I worked odd jobs, trying to make ends meet and keep my mom in heat and electricity. I felt the pull to follow my brother, I'll admit it. I even went out with him on a job once. Seemed like easy money. Until someone got arrested or killed.

Somehow I rallied. I sent out a hundred more résumés and finally got a call to come downtown for an interview for a low-level government job. I wore the only suit I had, which I'd dug out of the back of Mom's closet. I didn't know if it was my dad's or someone else's, but the jacket fit. Pants were a bit long, so I folded them up a little and taped them to the inside of the pant legs with duct tape. I shined my shoes as best I could and then bummed a ride downtown with my closest neighbor, an older lady about six lots down to the east.

Mrs. Randolph stopped the car at the empty county building.

"Here you go, Kenny."

"No, it's not here, Mrs. Randolph. It's in the Guardian Building."

"You said Wayne County."

"Yes, but the offices moved to the Guardian Building like six years ago."

She looked perplexed but started up the car again.

I looked up past the For Sale sign in front of the imposing columned façade to the regal carved horses on the roof of the county building. They looked wild-eyed and barely tamed, straining against the reins held by impassive stone figures.

The car moved on slowly as Mrs. Randolph doubled back to Griswold Street. I thanked her and got out, then waved as she drove off. The enormous entrance to the Guardian Building was inlaid with a colorful mosaic and flanked by three-story-high native figures in shallow relief. Before I pushed through the door I took two deep breaths and I was glad I did because the soaring lobby stole the air from my lungs. It looked like a cathedral inside a giant kaleidoscope.

After a moment or two, I made it past the ornate lobby, into the elevators, and up to the desk in the appointed office on the ninth floor. But that was as far as I got. After talking with someone on the phone, the receptionist dismissed me as gently as she could. The position had been filled by the guy ahead of me. I thought of the phone call days before when I had chosen the later timeslot to be sure I wouldn't be late for the interview. Then I turned around and staggered out.

My ride home wouldn't be coming for another hour, so I wandered down the street and found myself staring at a flight of steps up to a train platform. I climbed the stairs and pulled some change out of my pocket. I went through the turnstile to the waiting area and leaned against the wall for a few minutes before the People Mover slid into place.

Inside, I sat down on a blue vinyl seat and twisted around to look out the window behind me.

As Detroit whizzed by outside, I sunk further and further into my own self, squeezing shut the space that my hope had occupied just minutes before. My dreams had forgotten me—and now all I could think about was how much I wanted to forget them. How could my teachers have been so careless?

Fifteen minutes or so later, the glittering glass towers of the Renaissance Center filled my field of vision. Another dead dream. Too much ambition. Too much hope. Who could ever fulfill those expectations?

The train stopped at the Millender Center station and an old man stepped on. Though there were plenty of open seats, he sat in the one to my immediate left. He smelled strongly of sweat and stale cigarettes and his gray hair looked like it hadn't been washed in months. I almost moved, but my stop was next anyway.

When the train slowed at the Financial District station, I stood up.

"Wait a minute, young fella," came the raspy voice from beside me. "Ride with me a little while."

Something made me hesitate as I looked down into his sunken brown eyes. He looked so familiar, but I couldn't place him. I hesitated a moment too long. The doors closed and the train moved on. I sat back down.

"How you doing, old man?" I asked.

"Oh, I'm all right. Better than you are, I think."

"Why do you say that?"

"I know what disappointment looks like."

Beneath his ragged beard, his face was deeply lined and brown, but I couldn't tell if it was from genetics or the sun. The chapped hands that rested on his thin legs looked like they'd known hard work and bitter cold. I self-consciously tucked my own smooth hands into my pockets.

"Been a hard day?" he pried.

"Yeah, you could say that."

"Want to talk about it?"

"No."

He smiled at that and I could see that he was missing a few key teeth and the ones he still had were a dingy yellow from a lifetime of smoking.

"Suit yourself. Just thought maybe I could help you out."

"Yeah? How's talking to you about my problems going to help me out?"

"Well, that depends. Sometimes just talking makes people feel better. And sometimes people just need a little *extra* help."

"Help with what?"

"Forgetting."

For the second time that day I stopped breathing. I did know this man. Knew him inside and out. He was the thing I'd been chasing before I started chasing my dreams.

"You're the Memory Man?" I asked, afraid that when I said it he might just disappear in a puff of smoke.

"I guess that's what they call me."

I looked at him through narrowed eyes.

"How do I know it's really you?"

"I guess you don't. Not right now, anyway. But if you've got something that needs forgetting, you could test me out."

My mind raced through the past, through all of the hurt and betrayal and embarrassment of my young life. I could picture the notebook full of clues about the Memory Man sitting in the bottom of my desk drawer in that second story bedroom at my mom's house. I thought of my list of things to forget, which had grown to be many pages long. I thought of my big dreams about a job that would get me out of this town. And I knew exactly what I needed to forget. That old guy found me just in the nick of time.

I opened my mouth, ready to spill my guts. Ready to tell this old man about my ambition, my impossible dream of greatness. Ready to let it all be wiped from my mind, never to return. Then I remembered what that lost woman yelled as I ran off to find the Memory Man almost ten years earlier. *Be careful what you tell him.*

The old man bored into me with those brown eyes and I wondered if somehow he already knew.

I shut my mouth.

"You know, old man, I don't think you can help me."

"Not convinced I'm the real thing?"

"It's not that. I believe you. But I don't think I need your services."

He looked skeptical.

"If you'd found me when I was a kid, I would have had a lot to tell you. We could have had a weekly appointment and you probably could have made a lot of money off me. But now…thanks, but no thanks. No offense."

He shook his head. "None taken, young man. Though you know you're the first person who's ever said no."

I wasn't sure what to say to that, but then I didn't have to say anything. The train stopped and the Memory Man stood up. He walked to the open door.

"Maybe I'll see you around," he said.

"Maybe," I said.

The door closed behind him and the train zipped along. Eventually I got off, sat on a bench, and waited for my ride.

That night I got Mom to bed and went up to my room. Sitting at my little childhood desk, I flipped through my notebook and scanned the map and read through my long list of bad memories. For just a moment, I wondered if I'd made the right decision. But I then realized that I truly didn't want to forget anything. Because it all made me who I am today, no matter how bad it was. And even when a dream doesn't become a reality, you can't live without hope.

Now I gaze out that same window that me and Mike looked out when I first heard of the Memory Man, only there are no lights left on my street. Houses all empty or gone. Streetlights all burned out or broke or stolen and sold for scrap. Nothing but black.

Still, in the distance I can see a couple houses with the lights on. And up above the sky is filled with stars that the feeble light below can no longer blot out. They've always been there; I just couldn't see them before.

Detroit was built by people who dreamed big, worked hard, and didn't wait for someone to hand them success—people who made their fair share of bad memories. Everybody had hard times. Even in the glory days.

I don't want to forget what made us so great—or what brought us so low. I need the past.

Because forgetting is for the weak.

ABOUT THE AUTHOR

ERIN BARTELS is a copywriter and editor by day, a novelist by night, and a poet, painter, and photographer in between. In 2015, she was a finalist for the Rising Star Award from the Women's Fiction Writers Association, and in 2014 she was a finalist in *The Saturday Evening Post* Great American Fiction Contest. She is also the author of *The Intentional Writer*. A member of the Capital City Writers Association and the Women's Fiction Writers Association, she is the features editor for WFWA's quarterly newsletter.

She lives with her husband, Zachary, and their son in a little old brick house in Michigan's capital city, nestled somewhere between angry protesters on the Capitol lawn and couch-burning frat boys at nearby Michigan State University. And yet, she claims it is really quite peaceful.

She is on Facebook @ErinBartelsAuthor, Twitter @ErinLBartels, and Instagram @erinbartelswrites.

Stop wishing.
Start writing.

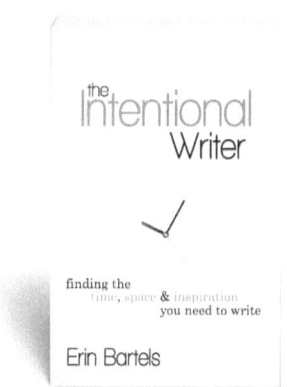

Do you wish you had the time to write?

Do you find it difficult to even carve out a space for yourself in your hustle-and-bustle household?

Do you feel like all of your inspiration and creativity is being sucked up by tasks you don't even enjoy?

The Intentional Writer was written for you.

- Analyze your motivations for writing
- Keep your ideas flowing
- Handle internal and external distractions
- Reshape your surroundings and your schedule to aid your process
- Take your work from first draft to final publishable product

Visit www.ErinBartels.com/books to purchase.

Understory Press